PLANET DIVOC 91

CREDITS

CHAPTER 1:
TRANSPARENCY IS FOR WINDOWS

Art: Charlie Adlard
Words: Sara Kenney
Colours: James Devlin
Lettering: Hassan Otsmane-Elhaou
Cover: Elsa Charretier

CHAPTER 2:
THE REAL QUESTION

Art: Nick Brokenshire
Words: Charlotte Bailey
Colours: James Devlin
Letters: Hassan Otsmane-Elhaou
Cover: Matt Kindt

CHAPTER 3:
EEDYATS IN EVERY GALAXY

Art & Words: Hannah Berry
Colours: James Devlin
Letters: Hassan Otsmane-Elhaou
Cover: VV Glass

WELCOME TO PLANET DIVOC BY SARA KENNEY

Hello and welcome. I'm Sara, writer & co-lead on this participatory arts project. I've spent a good chunk of my career working on science fiction and 'what if' scenarios for TV, comics and immersive experiences but, like most, was not prepared for what happened in March 2020. When lockdown hit, I was working with Bella Starling, Head of Public Programmes at Vocal, part of Manchester NHS Trust, and it became obvious that our thinking should be refocused on the pandemic. We quickly realised there was a ton of practical information about Covid-19 out there, but that it was difficult to know who to trust and there were virtually no young and diverse voices in the mix. So we started canvassing the views of 16- to 25-year-olds from around the world to help think about what was needed.

The project started as a series of comic strips and participatory workshops and grew into a full-length exquisite corpse comic, artwork, poetry, articles, music playlists and films created with input from artists, scientists, musicians and young people from around the globe.

The young people's voices are key to this project. That was one of the main ambitions: to act as a space to think together about how we move forward and create a more positive future. So all the art and stories in this project were created during 2020, at the height of the pandemic, and it's fascinating to have captured all those ideas and emotions in this way.

I think it's important to talk a bit about the outcomes. We worked hard to examine the emerging narratives surrounding the pandemic, like the use of military metaphors, impact of Black Lives Matter (BLM), vaccine hesitancy vs anti-vax, the role of historians and social scientists, and so on. We interrogated the positive and negative and shared these views with scientists and policy makers. Through a process of 50+ workshops we created a 10-point manifesto, which articulated some of our ideas for change, and they can be found at the end of the comic and at our website www.planetdivoc91.com.

We were able to share our views with Independent Sage, MQ Mental Health Research, Office for National Statistics, Wellcome Trust, UK Research and Innovation (UKRI), World Health Organisation (WHO) and many others. The young adults contributed to the Academy of Medical Sciences' 2021 'Winter Report for UK Government'. They also presented to scientists including UK Chief Medical Officer Professor Chris Whitty at a major conference 'Progress and priorities for mental health sciences research since Covid-19'. The team in India interviewed the Principal Scientific Adviser to the Government of India, Professor VijayRaghavan, and the team in South Africa shared their thoughts on national breakfast TV show, *The Expresso Show*. It's impossible to fully measure the impact, but we're hopeful we made a difference.

Finally, I think it's a mistake not to value and include our artists, musicians and storytellers when thinking about global health. Their ability to creatively share ideas, visualise solutions and re-imagine our world in more positive ways is vital. So I want to thank all the comic creators and musicians who joined us on this journey.

As a team we continue to collaborate in various capacities. Collective working on a global scale was profoundly rewarding on many levels. It's over two years since the first lockdown and we're still working with many of the young people. Their ideas and enthusiasm were a beacon for the team and, quite honestly, I can't wait for them to be in charge of this planet...

Hope you enjoy the comic, music, art, films and articles as much as we enjoyed creating them!

CHAPTER 1:
TRANSPARENCY IS FOR WINDOWS

Art: Charlie Adlard
Words: Sara Kenney
Colours: James Devlin
Letters: Hassan Otsmane-Elhaou
Cover: Elsa Charretier

WHAT'S WRONG WITH HER?

HER NAME? SANDA. SHE'S 23, SHE'S MY BIG SISTER.
I SAID ALREADY, I'M 19.

MY DAYS, IS SHE HAVING A SEIZURE?

HELP HER! PLEASE!
WHOOOSH
SHE'S COMING 'ROUND.
THIS IS ALWAYS THE TOUGH PART, WHEN WE LET THEM OUT.
AFTER ALL THIS TIME...

THEY'LL ADAPT, THEY ALWAYS DO. MOST OF THEM ANYWAY...
EUGHHH, YOUR FACES ARE WELL WARPED.

RUDE.
SHE'S IN SHOCK.
SANDA, YOU REMEMBER WHAT THEY TOLD US RIGHT?

SOMETHING ABOUT... AN EVAC?
WE GOT TAKEN TO A SAFE PLANET AND--

C'MON, GET INVOLVED, THIS IS PROPER EXCITING.
Board of Adversity Scientists for Intergalactic Leadership (BASIL)
YOU SHOULD ALL HAVE YOUR PLANET DIVOC-91 WELCOME PACKS.
Board of Adversity Scientists for Galactic Leadership (B

WE AT BASIL WORK TO PROTECT SPECIES AT RISK FROM EXTINCTION LEVEL EVENTS.

HOW DID WE EVEN GET HERE?

13

IT'S CALLED ZAPPING AND--
THE DETAILS ARE TOO COMPLICATED FOR YOUR BRAIN ARCHITECTURE.
WHY CAN'T YOU TELL US WHAT THIS EXTINCTION LEVEL EVENT IS?
AND THEN ZAP AWAY THE DANGER?
AND WHY NOT ZAP OLDER ADULTS HERE, OR LITTLE KIDS?

PLEASE, HOMO SAPIENS. DETAILED PLANS ARE IN YOUR WELCOME PACK.
THIS IS ALL FOR YOUR OWN GOOD.

NOPE, NOT FEELING GOOD RIGHT NOW.
I'VE READ THE PACK, ALL SEEMS LEGIT.

THEY'RE HIDING SOMETHING.
ARE THEY GONNA EXPERIMENT ON US?
OR TAKE RESOURCES FROM OUR PLANET?

SOUNDS LIKE YOUR QUOTING FROM MA'S WHATSAPP GROUPS, CHILL!
WE'RE HERE TO ENSURE THE SURVIVAL OF HOMO SAPIENS, LIKE A DNA BANK I GUESS?

HEY, ISN'T THAT ARAMINTA LOVE FROM THE QUANTUM SPARK PLUG FILMS?
DISTANT YET CLOSE. FAR YET NEAR.
Board of A
Intergal
OMETH
KUM BA YA MY LORD, KUM BA YA.
LET'S SHARE WITH THE HEROES BACK HOME. SING FOR THEM, BAKE FOR THEM--

CHOMP!
NOOO!
DID THAT PLANT JUST EAT ARAMINTA LOVE?
YES, YES IT DID.
SHE WAS RUINING A GREAT AFRICAN AMERICAN FOLK SONG...

WE'RE LEAVING NOW!

GOTTA GET TO HIGHER GROUND, TRY AND CONTACT EARTH.
I MEAN, WE'RE LIGHT-YEARS AWAY, BUT WHATEVS...

WHY CAN'T THEY JUST TELL US WHAT'S GOING ON?
ADRO ALWAYS SAYS TRANSPARENCY IS FOR WINDOWS.
HE'S THE HEAD OF BASIL, PROMOTED FOR ALL THE WRONG REASONS.
RUN!
THE NEWCOMERS NEVER TAKE TO YOU, TENDAI. DO THEY?

NO SIGNAL.
I CAN'T TAKE THIS CHAMPO. WHERE ARE WE? WHAT'S GOING TO HAPPEN TO US?

PERHAPS YOU'RE ASKING THE WRONG QUESTIONS?

WHAT DO YOU MEAN?
WHERE DO YOU WANT TO GO?
WHAT DO YOU WANT TO HAPPEN?

HARRI'S A HISTORIAN AND PHILOSOPHER-- THEY SPEAK IN TONGUES.
OF COURSE, BOBBIE THE REDUCTIVE SCIENTIST, YOU'D START WITH THE FACTS.
PROBLEM IS WE DON'T HAVE ALL THE FACTS!

WHAT THEY GOING ON 'BOUT?

21

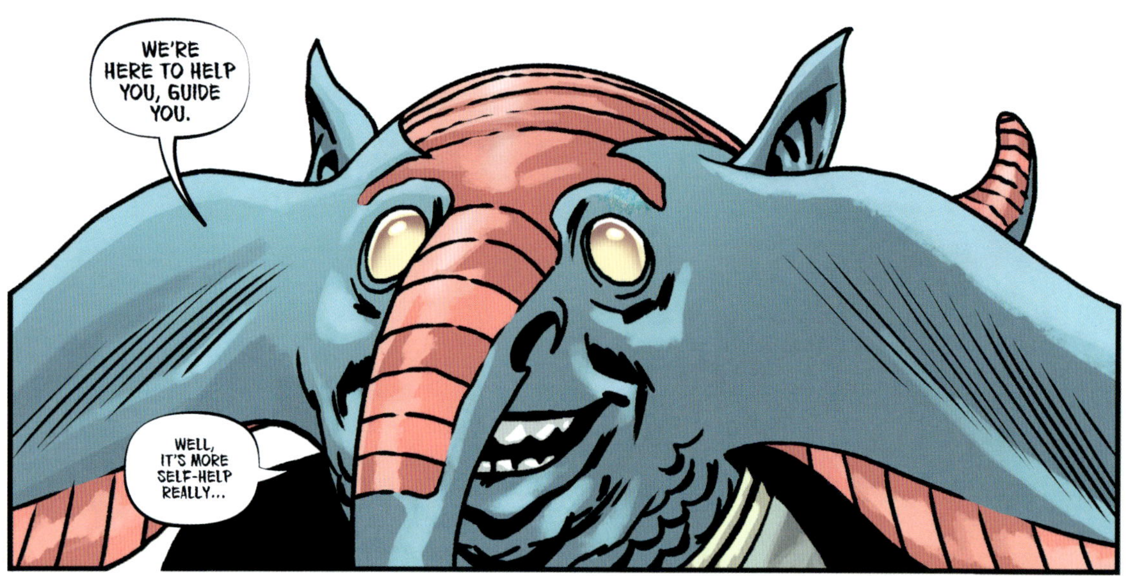

WE'RE HERE TO HELP YOU, GUIDE YOU.
WELL, IT'S MORE SELF-HELP REALLY...

STOP, EVERYONE. LET'S JUST SHARE THE DATA WITH THEM.
OH YES, I LOVE DATA.

CHAMPO, YOU HAVE BEEN CHOSEN. YOU'RE ONE OF THE FEW WITH THE INTELLECT WE CAN USE.
SOUNDS ABOUT RIGHT. NAH MATE, WE'RE NOT STAYING.

AAARGGGHH!
ARAMINTA, WHAT THE...?

COME TOGETHER AS ONE!
SHE GOT BITTEN BY A SMASH PLANT?
SMASH PLANT? WHAT THE HELL IS THAT?
THEY TAKE YOUR WORST ANXIETIES AND RECONFIGURE YOU INTO A WALKING MANIFESTATION OF ALL THAT FEAR.

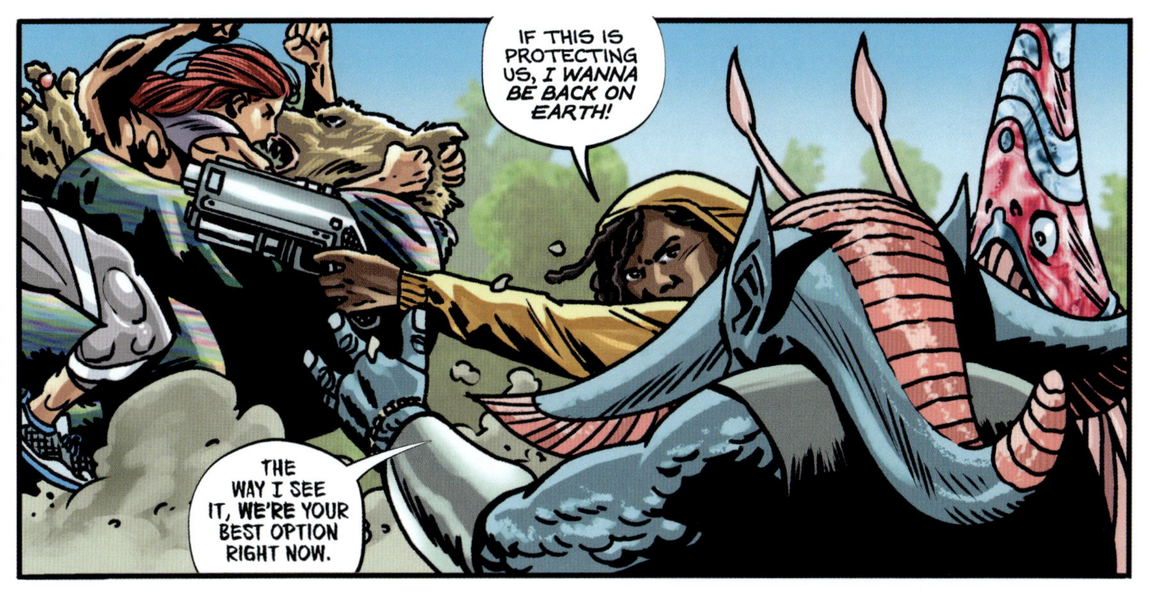

IF THIS IS PROTECTING US, I WANNA BE BACK ON EARTH!
THE WAY I SEE IT, WE'RE YOUR BEST OPTION RIGHT NOW.

BOOM

OH NO, AND IT'S TIME YOU STOP AND LISTEN TO WHAT WE GOTTA SAY ABOUT OUR OPTIONS.

CHAPTER 2:
THE REAL QUESTION
Art: Nick Brokenshire
Words: Charlotte Bailey
Colours: James Devlin
Letters: Hassan Otsmane-Elhaou
Cover: Matt Kindt

WHY PROLONG THE INEVITABLE? THEY'LL FIND OUT EVENTUALLY.
FIND OUT WHAT?
...THEY DESERVE THE TRUTH.
I'M WORRIED ABOUT TELLING YOU THIS, BUT AN ASTEROID IS ON COURSE TO HIT YOUR HOME PLANET, CAUSING AN EXTINCTION LEVEL EVENT.
WE WANTED YOU ALL TO FEEL SAFE HERE BEFORE EXPOSING YOU TO MORE CONCERNING CHANGES.
YOU'RE HERE FOR YOUR OWN GOOD--
I'VE HEARD ENOUGH! CHAMPO, LET'S GO.

SERIOUSLY? THAT IS NEVER GOING TO WORK.
I'VE TRIED TO TELL HER. SHE'D NEED DOCTOR WHO'S SUPERPHONE FOR INTERSTELLAR COMMUNICATION.
I THINK YOU'LL FIND THAT A SUBSPACE RADIO WOULD DO.
OH YEAHHH, LIKE THE HYPERCHANNEL IN STAR TREK.
CHAMPO! STOP FRATERNISING WITH THE ALIENS! STRANGER DANGER!
DO THEY LOOK DANGEROUS TO YOU?
IF THEY WERE UP TO NO GOOD, DO YOU THINK THEY'D TELL US STRAIGHT?
OF COURSE NOT.
ACTUALLY...

...THERE IS SOMETHING ELSE WE HAVEN'T TOLD YOU.
FOLLOW ME.
A HOSPITAL?
I KNEW IT!
THIS IS WHERE YOU'RE CONDUCTING EXPERIMENTS ON HUMANS...

ARE THESE...
...ALIEN CHILDREN?
WHAT'S WRONG WITH THEM? WHY ISN'T ANYONE HELPING THEM?
THE REAL QUESTION IS: HOW CAN WE HELP THEM?
THEY HAVE A STRANGE SICKNESS WHICH HAS ALTERED THEIR MOOD. THEY NO LONGER LAUGH OR PLAY LIKE LITTLE CHILDREN...
...IT'S AS IF ALL OF THEIR JOY EVAPORATED OVERNIGHT.
WE ARE WORKING ON A CURE. HOWEVER, THIS ILLNESS IS CONTAGIOUS--
--EXCEPT FOR HUMANS. WE BELIEVE IT'S SAFE FOR YOU.

...WE NEED VOLUNTEERS TO--
NO, NO, NO. I CANNOT HANDLE THIS RIGHT NOW.
ALL I WANT IS MY BED AND WIFI. I DON'T UNDERSTAND ANY OF THIS CRAZY STUFF. I WANT TO GO HOME.
WWW. MIXCLOUD.COM/ PlanetDivoc91
THERE IS MUCH WE DON'T KNOW, NOR CAN CONTROL. WHETHER IT BE DISPLACEMENT, EXTINCTION, OR WHETHER TO TRUST A STRANGER.
YOU CAN ONLY KNOW HOW YOU FEEL...
...AND YOU CAN ONLY CONTROL WHAT YOU DO ABOUT IT.

FAKE NEWS OR NOT, SOMETHING SERIOUS IS UP WITH THESE KIDS!
I KNOW THAT CHAMPO, DON'T GET ALL PREACHY!
WHAT DO YOU NEED US TO DO?

CHAPTER 3:
EEDYATS IN EVERY GALAXY
Art & Words: Hannah Berry
Colours: James Devlin
Letters: Hassan Otsmane-Elhaou
Cover: VV Glass

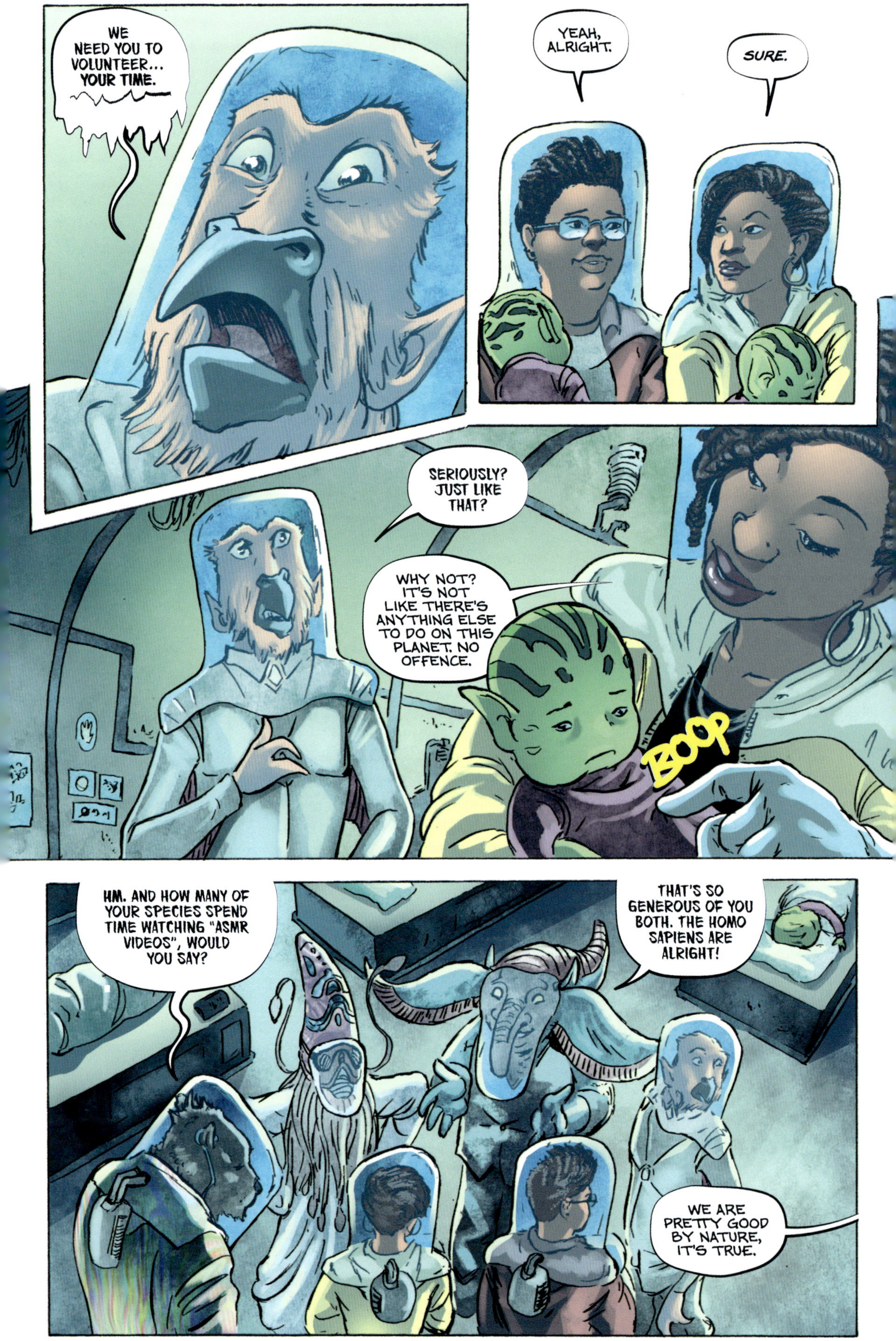

WE NEED YOU TO VOLUNTEER... YOUR TIME.
YEAH, ALRIGHT.
SURE.
SERIOUSLY? JUST LIKE THAT?
WHY NOT? IT'S NOT LIKE THERE'S ANYTHING ELSE TO DO ON THIS PLANET. NO OFFENCE.
BOOP
HM. AND HOW MANY OF YOUR SPECIES SPEND TIME WATCHING "ASMR VIDEOS", WOULD YOU SAY?
THAT'S SO GENEROUS OF YOU BOTH. THE HOMO SAPIENS ARE ALRIGHT!
WE ARE PRETTY GOOD BY NATURE, IT'S TRUE.

AH, DR. MALULEKE! THESE HUMANS HAVE AGREED TO VOLUNTEER THEIR TIME--
YOU'RE A HUMAN!
YOU'RE A DINNER LADY?

HAIBO! HUMAN, YES. DINNER LADY, NO.
THERE WAS SOME CONFUSION WHEN I ASKED FOR A LAB COAT.

WEIRD TO SEE A HUMAN OVER 25 HERE!
JA, ABOUT THAT--
DR. MALULEKE WAS ONE OF THE ADVANCE PARTY BROUGHT TO CONSULT ON THIS VIRUS. SHE HAS BEEN MOST GENEROUS WITH HER TIME.
MOST GENEROUS.

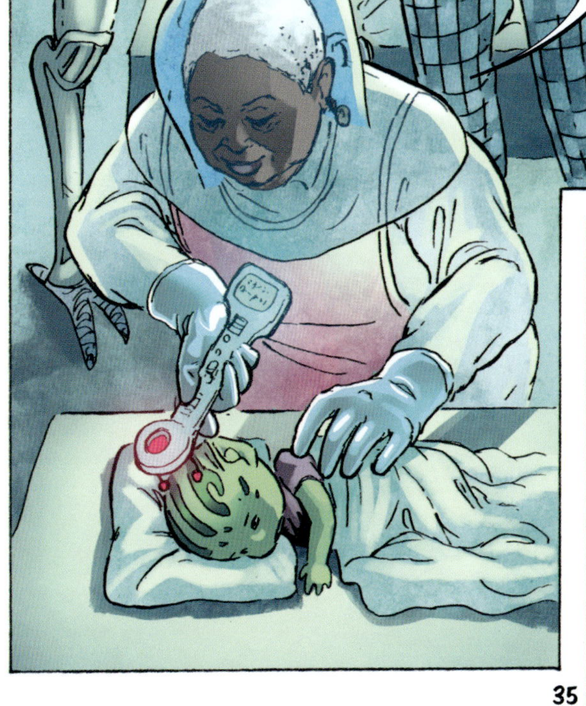

WELL... CONSIDERING WHERE THE VIRUS CAME FROM...

...TURNS OUT THERE'S A STRANGE PARALLEL IN ALL OF OUR GENETIC CODING...
...WHICH COULD BE AN ARGUMENT FOR CREATIONISM OR PANSPERMIA IF YOU'RE INTO EITHER OF THOSE THEORIES.
I DON'T KNOW WHAT 'PANSPERMIA' IS, BUT MAYBE NOT IN FRONT OF THE KIDS, EH?

UHHH, ARE THEY OKAY?!
OH NO...NOT AGAIN...
WAAAAH!
WAAAAH!

RUN THE SOPORIFATE!
THE SOPORIFATE!!!
WAAAH! WAAAH! WAAAH!

Waaah!
WHAT'S HAPPENING?! WHAT ARE THEY DOING?!
THE VIRUS HAS THESE PSYCHOSOMATIC EFFECTS WE JUST DON'T UNDERSTAND--
Waaah!
WE DON'T KNOW WHY THEY DO THIS, BUT THEY ALL DO IT SIMULTANEOUSLY, EVEN WHEN WE ISOLATE THEM!
MAKE THEM STOP!
Waaah!
Waaah!
WE'RE TRYING! HOLD ON...

WHAT. THE. ACTUAL...?
EISH... WE DON'T UNDERSTAND IT. WE CAN'T PREDICT IT. YET.
IT JUST HAPPENS.

BUT AT LEAST WE KNOW HOW TO CURE THEM NOW! FOLLOW ME.
AND BRING A COUPLE OF PATIENTS, WOULD YOU?

YOU SHOULD PROBABLY KNOW THERE'S A BIT OF A STIGMA AROUND VOLUNTEERS...THEY CAN BE TREATED WITH...
...WOULD YOU SAY SUSPICION?
CONTEMPT?
FEAR?
TCH. EEDYATS IN EVERY GALAXY.
SO, WAIT, IF YOU KNOW HOW TO CURE THEM, WHY ARE THEY STILL--
--WHAT THE HELL IS THAT?

THIS IS 'THE TRANSFUSER'! WHO WANTS TO GO FIRST?

YOU ARE JOKING.
YOU DID EXPLAIN THIS PROCESS, DID YOU NOT?
WE ASKED IF THEY WANTED TO GIVE UP THEIR TIME... I THOUGHT THAT WAS PRETTY SELF-EXPLANATORY?
HUMAN TIME BEING THE MOST POTENT, ETC.

YEAH, 'GIVE UP OUR TIME'. AT NO POINT DID BEING HOOKED INTO TO R2D2'S HELLRAISER COUSIN COME UP.
AH, I SEE THE CONFUSION: YOUR ANTIBODIES CAN CURE THESE CHILDREN, BUT EACH TRANSFUSION SHAVES APPROXIMATELY ONE MONTH OFF YOUR LIFESPAN.

GIVE UP YOUR TIME, LIKE I DID...
...LITERALLY.

CHAPTER 4:
IT'S JUST A PHASE
Art & Words: Rachael Smith
Colours: James Devlin
Letters: Hassan Otsmane-Elhaou
Cover: Leslie Hung

YEWANDE
BLONDE

HAS SANDA TEXTED YET? I'M GONNA HAVE TO GO IN A MINUTE...

SHE'S NOT...BUT I'M TOTALLY FINE ON MY OWN, MUM. IF YOU NEED TO GO, GO.
I BET IT'S THAT NEW MANAGER KEEPING HER LATE AGAIN...
JINGLE JINGLE
AH!

HI--
THERE'S A PIZZA IN THE FREEZER SO MAYBE YOU COULD DO IT WITH SOME CHIPS AND BEANS FOR YOU AND YOUR SISTER'S TEA. I'M ON THE LATE SHIFT AGAIN SO I'LL NOT SEE YOU 'TIL THE MORNING.
CAFFE ZERO

WE'RE LIKE SHIPS IN THE NIGHT, EH!?

SLAM

≡SIGH≡ "HI, SANDA, HOW WAS YOUR SHIFT?"
WELL YOU HAVE TO GIVE ME A CHANCE TO ASK YOU!
CAFFE

NOT YOU-- MUM. BE NICE IF SHE WEREN'T SO BUSY, EH?
BE NICE IF SHE COULD LEARN I'M NOT YOUR SISTER...

...YOU KNOW SHE STRUGGLES WITH THAT, CHAMPO. IT'S LIKE A WHOLE NEW SORT OF CONCEPT FOR HER GENERATION.
I'M NON-BINARY NOT... NETFLIX...

PFFFFT-HAHAHA! I CAN'T BELIEVE SHE STILL HASN'T GOTTEN HER HEAD AROUND THAT!
"THERE ARE NO ADVERTS, SANDA! THIS CAN'T BE LEGAL! TURN IT OFF! TURN IT OFF!"
IT'S NOT FUNNY!

URGH!
CHAMPO!

YOU...UNGRATEFUL PIECE OF CRAP! DO YOU HAVE ANY IDEA HOW HARD ME AND MUM ARE WORKING JUST SO YOU CAN GO TO COLLEGE?! IT'S NOT LIKE I DIDN'T WANT TO GO, YOU KNOW! INSTEAD I'M SERVING COFFEES TO IDIOTS ALL DAY AND YOU'RE HERE RUINING YOUR HOMEWORK WITH YOUR HISSY FITS!
I NEVER ASKED EITHER OF YOU TO MAKE ALL THESE SACRIFICES! STOP THROWING THAT IN MY FACE! IT'S NOT LIKE I'D EVEN BE ABLE TO DO EITHER OF YOUR JOBS WITH MY STUPID LEG--OR HAD YOU BOTH FORGOTTEN ABOUT THAT?!

JINGLE JINGLE

CRAP! I BET MUM HEARD US ARGUING...HERE, YOU HIDE THESE IN YOUR BAG, I'LL GRAB A CLOTH.
OKAY, SANDA.

SANDAAA!? CHAMPOOO!?
OH...UH, ALRIGHT, MUM? DID YOU FORGET SOME--
CAFFE ZERO

SANDAAAAAA....CHAMPOOOOO...
MY GIRLS...TAKE YOUR MEDICINE...
IS JUST A PHAAAASE, CHAMPOOOOO...
JUST A PHAAAASE MY
LITTLE GIIIIRL...

MUM!?
WHAT...WHAT'S
HAPPENED?!
GET
BACK!
SHE MUST
HAVE BEEN
BITTEN BY
A SMASH
PLANT!

A...WHAT?
OH...NO...

...NO, NO
O NO NO NO
NO NO NO N
O NO NO NO
O NO

45

SANDA!
WAKE UP!
IT'S OK!

WE'RE
OKAY.

:GASP:
NO! NO!
NO!

IT'S GOOD
THAT YOU'RE
AWAKE THOUGH,
I SIGNED US UP
FOR HARVEST
DUTY!

YOU...WAIT,
WHAT?

WELL,
I JUST
THOUGHT YOU'D
PREFER TO DO
SOMETHING
RATHER THAN
SIT AROUND
BEING
BORED.

I HAVE LITERALLY NEVER, IN
MY WHOLE LIFE, HAD THE
OPPORTUNITY TO BE
BORED, CHAMPO.
I MIGHT HAVE
ENJOYED IT!

WHOA!
LOOK AT
THIS!

SANDA...
YEAH?

I KNOW YOU SAID WE SHOULD TAKE A COUPLE OF DAYS TO THINK ABOUT IT...BUT I WANT TO HELP THE BABY ALIENS.
CHAMPO! IT'S BEEN ONE NIGHT!

WE'VE BEEN PUT HERE FOR A REASON! WE CAN DO REAL GOOD! WE CAN HELP THESE CHILDREN!
YEAH BY GIVING UP YEARS OF OUR LIVES!

GIVING UP A SMALL PART OF OUR LIVES SO THAT OTHERS DON'T LOSE THE ENTIRETY OF THEIRS...I...I'M SURPRISED YOU'RE NOT FEELING THE SAME, SANDA.
BETWEEN HELPING MUM LOOK AFTER YOU, AND THEN GETTING A JOB AT SIXTEEN SO YOU COULD GO TO COLLEGE, I'VE ALREADY HAD TO GIVE UP MY CHILDHOOD... WHY SHOULD I GIVE UP MY TWENTIES AS WELL! AND FOR BLOODY ALIENS WHO WE DON'T EVEN KNOW!

HOW MANY TIMES DO I HAVE TO TELL YOU: I NEVER *ASKED* YOU TO DO THAT FOR ME! STOP THROWING THAT IN MY FACE! I NEVER EVEN *WANTED* THAT!
WELL THEN, WHAT THE HELL *DID* YOU WANT!?

ALL I EVER WANTED WAS TO LIVE IN A WORLD WHERE I'M NOT JUDGED FOR WHO I AM... I *HAVE* THAT HERE! THEY DON'T SEE *ANY* OF THAT!
HUMANS!

48

SEE? "HUMANS." ISN'T IT REFRESHING TO BE CALLED THAT?
HM. VERY PERSONABLE.

OH! ARE YOU...
HUMANS... YOU MUST COME WITH ME AT ONCE...
WHAT'S WRONG?

THE HOSPITAL... DR. MALULEKE... PLEASE... COME... AT ONCE.

CHAPTER 5:
MATURING

Art, Words & Colours: Karrie Fransman
Letters: Hassan Otsmane-Elhaou
Cover: Marco Finnegan

THE TRANSFUSER IS MALFUNCTIONING!
AND DR. MALULEKE IS...
...INSIDE.

DON'T TOUCH HER, SANDA

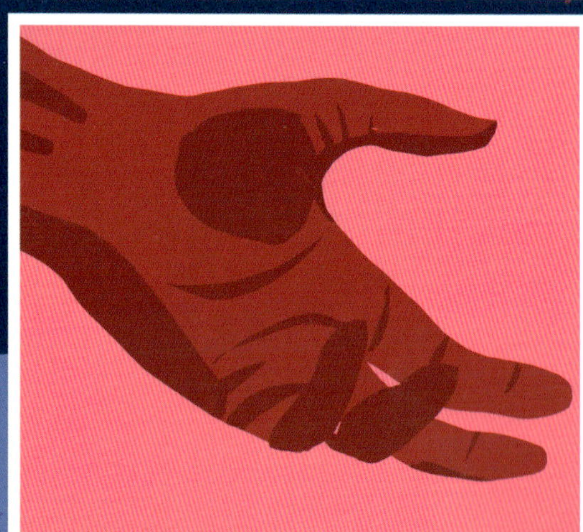

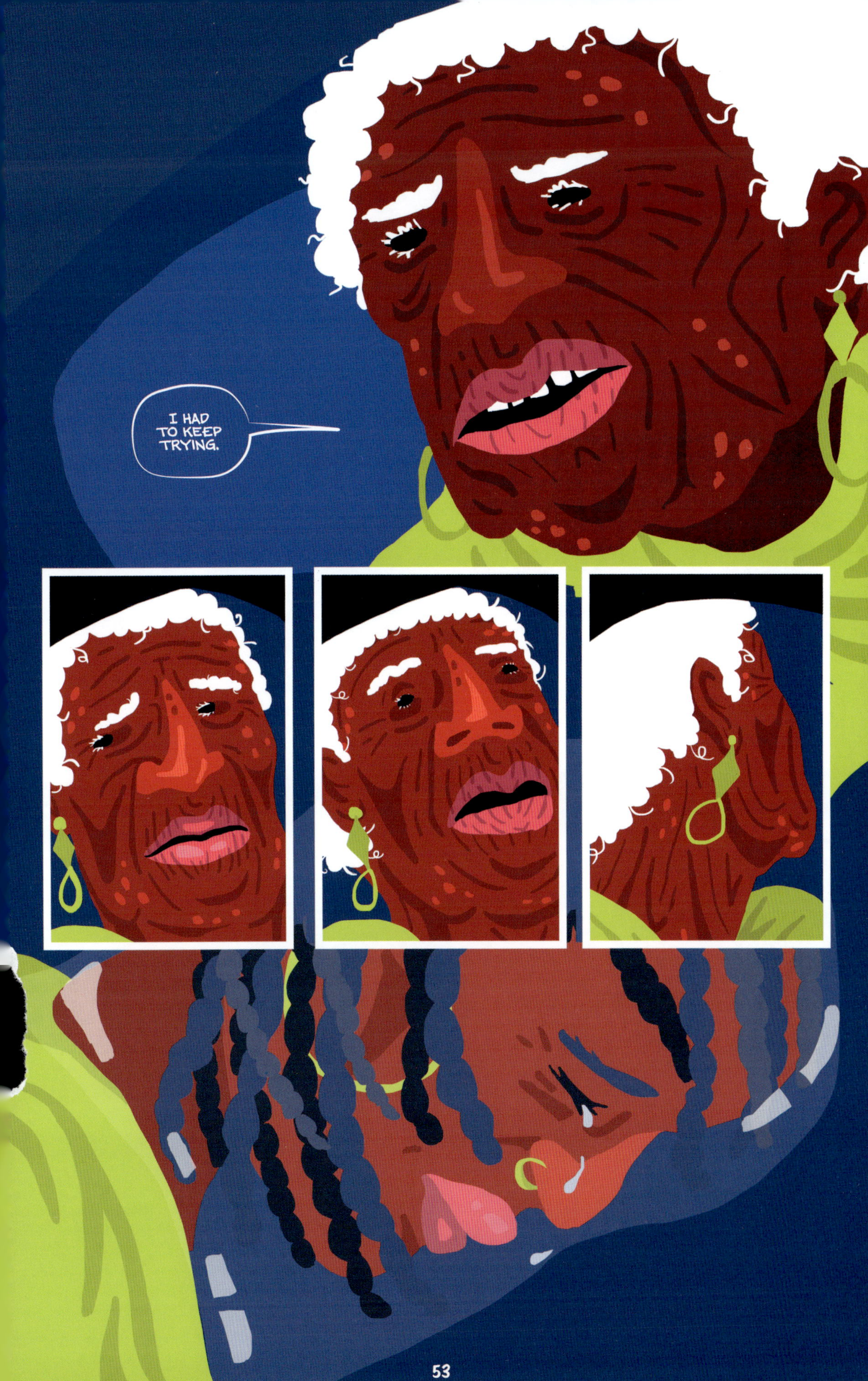

I HAD TO KEEP TRYING.

Later that night...
MAYBE I CAN GET MYSELF ONE OF THOSE LITTLE GLOVES MADONNA WEARS?

YOU ACTED WITH KINDNESS.
I LIKE TO COME UP HERE AND OBSERVE YOU HUMANS. YOU ALL RESPOND SO DIFFERENTLY.

SEE, THEY ARE QUEUING TO TRY AND CONTACT THEIR FAMILY ON THE SUBSPACE RADIO.
THEY MIGHT BE WAITING FOR WEEKS.

UGH. I REALLY NEED TO RING MY MUM.
OTHERS HAVE DIFFERENT COPING MECHANISMS.

WHOOP! YEAH, LADIES! LET'S DO OUR BIT TO STOP THE EXTINCTION OF THE HUMAN RACE.
EVERYONE ON EARTH IS GOING TO BE CRUSHED BY AN ASTEROID, YOU INSENSITIVE CREEP.

WHAT'S THAT NOISE?
KLAP
KLAP
KLAP

KLAP
KLAP
KLAP
KLAP
WE ARE HONOURING DR. MALULEKE.
SHE HAD HER SUSPICIONS.
WHAT HAPPENED TO HER?
SHE'D STARTED INSISTING WE ALL WORE FULL PPE.
THEN TODAY THE RESULTS CAME BACK.
THE VIRUS ORIGINATED IN HUMANS.

SHE WAS SO DETERMINED TO TRY AND FIND A CURE FOR HER PATIENTS, BUY THEM AS MUCH TIME AS POSSIBLE.
NO ONE KNEW THE TRANSFUSION WOULD BE HER LAST.
SHE SACRIFICED EVERYTHING FOR THEM.
IT APPEARS YOU MAY HAVE A LITTLE OF HER IN YOU.
WHICH IS WHY WE NEED YOUR HELP.
WHEN THE WORD GETS OUT THAT HUMANS WERE SPREADING THIS VIRUS...SOME WILL WANT REVENGE.

CHAPTER 6:
SAME BUT DIFFERENT

Art: Anand RK
Words: Nabeel Petersen
Colours: James Devlin
Letters: Hassan Otsmane-Elhaou
Cover: FØK

THOSE MEAT-EATERS PLANNED THIS. THEY'RE ABDUCTING OUR CHILDREN.
HOW COULD BASIL ALLOW THIS?

THERE IS NO VIRUS. THEY TRICKED US.
THE HUMANS ARE WEARING OUR CHILDREN'S SKINS SO THEY CAN INFILTRATE US.

NV FUNK
HUMANS WANT US AS THEIR SLAVES. THEY'RE TAKING OVER DIVOC-91.
THEY WANT TO TRANSFORM DIVOC-91 INTO EARTH!

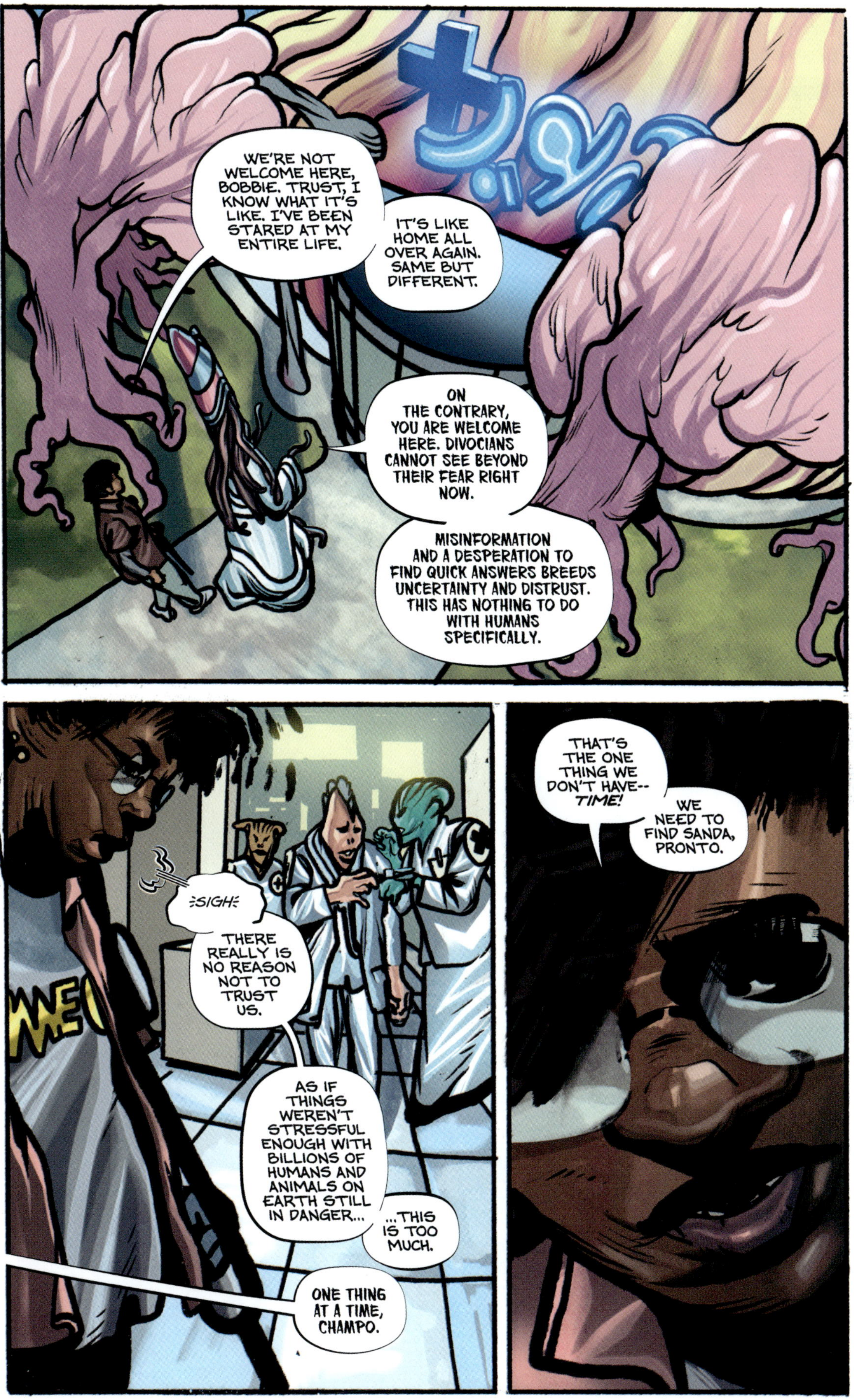

WE'RE NOT WELCOME HERE, BOBBIE. TRUST, I KNOW WHAT IT'S LIKE. I'VE BEEN STARED AT MY ENTIRE LIFE.
IT'S LIKE HOME ALL OVER AGAIN. SAME BUT DIFFERENT.
ON THE CONTRARY, YOU ARE WELCOME HERE. DIVOCIANS CANNOT SEE BEYOND THEIR FEAR RIGHT NOW.
MISINFORMATION AND A DESPERATION TO FIND QUICK ANSWERS BREEDS UNCERTAINTY AND DISTRUST. THIS HAS NOTHING TO DO WITH HUMANS SPECIFICALLY.
=SIGH=
THERE REALLY IS NO REASON NOT TO TRUST US.
AS IF THINGS WEREN'T STRESSFUL ENOUGH WITH BILLIONS OF HUMANS AND ANIMALS ON EARTH STILL IN DANGER...
...THIS IS TOO MUCH.
ONE THING AT A TIME, CHAMPO.

THAT'S THE ONE THING WE DON'T HAVE-- TIME!
WE NEED TO FIND SANDA, PRONTO.

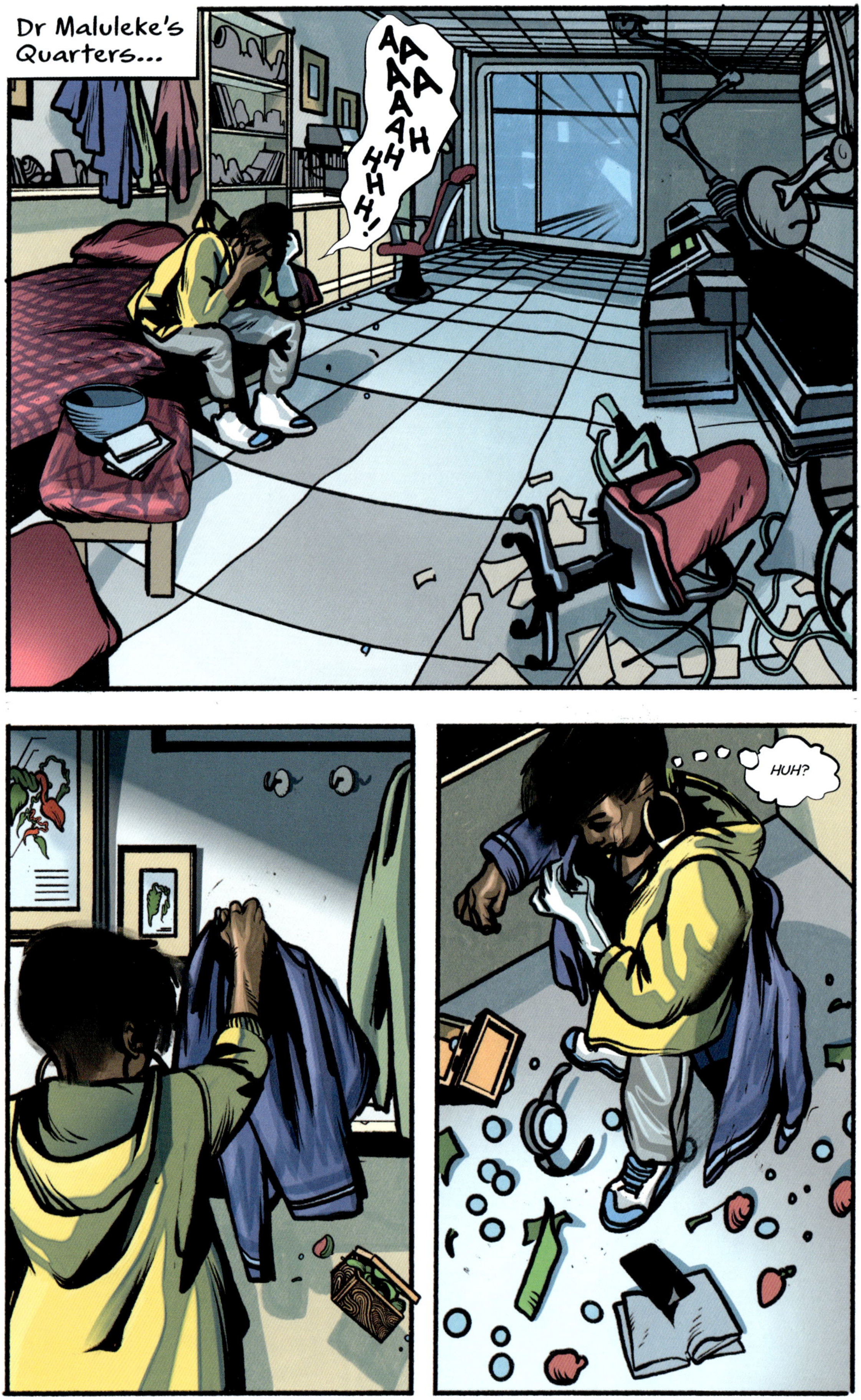

Dr Maluleke's Quarters...

AAAAAAHHHH!

HUH?

MONTH 1...
MONTH 4...
MONTH 9...
MONTH 12...
WHAT?! MALULEKE WAS ONLY TWO YEARS OLDER THAN ME!
HOW MANY CHILDREN DID SHE SAVE?

THERE YOU ARE! IT'S SCARY OUT THERE, SANDA. ALIENS ARE PLANNING A REVOLT AGAINST HUMANS!
THEY WANT US OUT!

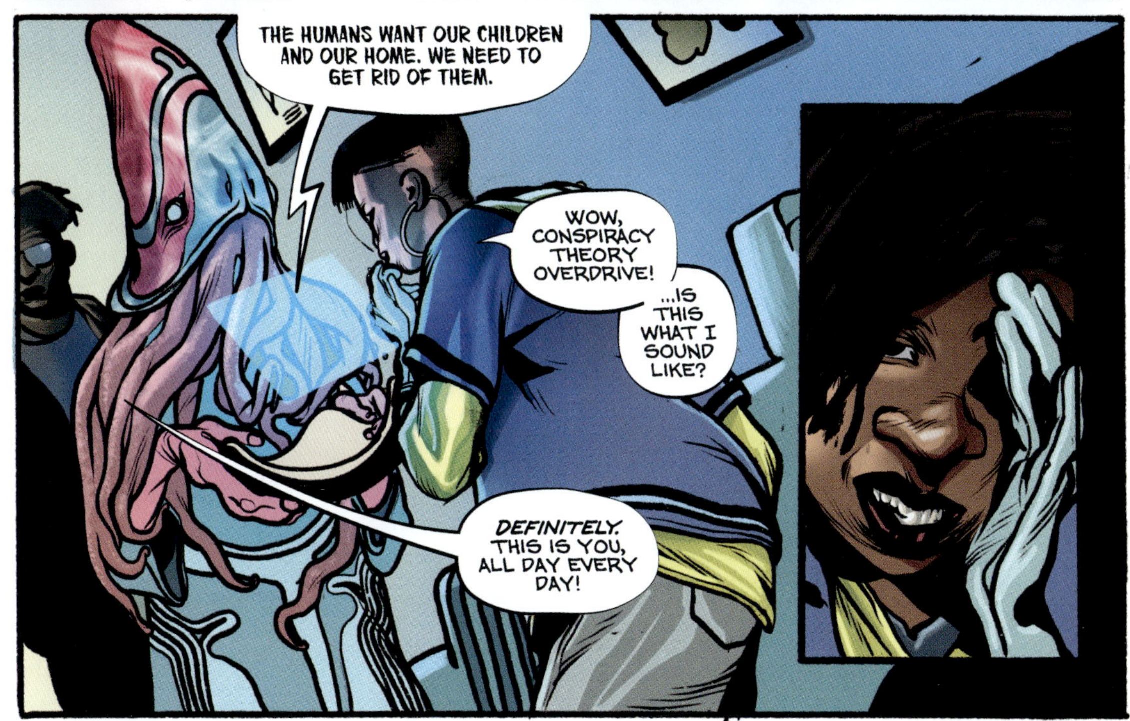

THE HUMANS WANT OUR CHILDREN AND OUR HOME. WE NEED TO GET RID OF THEM.
WOW, CONSPIRACY THEORY OVERDRIVE!
...IS THIS WHAT I SOUND LIKE?
DEFINITELY. THIS IS YOU, ALL DAY EVERY DAY!

Maluleke. Research Notes. Day 317.
My gut says the SMASH Plant holds some answers.
It may have caused the virus. A manifestation of BASIL's fears.
I believe BASIL's worst fear is that humans may disrupt this planet's ecosystem and jeopardize the future of Divoc-91 and its people.

BOBBIE!
CHAMPO!
YOU HAVE TO SEE THIS!

CHAPTER 7:
CRISIS OF
EXISTENTIAL SELVES
Art: Zara Slattery
Words: Bobby Joseph
Colours: James Devlin
Letters: Hassan Otsmane-Elhaou
Cover: David Rubin

WHAT THE FUDGING CAKE?

THIS IS THE FORTIES COMIC BOOK VERSION OF YOU. SHE'S THE DUMB SERVANT TYPE OR SIDEKICK TO THE HEROIC 'WHITE SAVIOUR'. PEOPLE OF COLOUR WERE ALWAYS PORTRAYED LIKE THAT, THE COMEDIC ELEMENT PLAYING UP TO RACIAL STEREOTYPES.
WELL MISS SANDA, I FELL DOWN SUM STAIR TODAY, MY DRAWS WERE IN THE AIR AND THEN I GOTTA SCARED BY SUM GHOST. WOULD YOU LIKE SOME FOOD?
ERR. NO THANKS! WOW, BLACK PEOPLE WERE WRITTEN WITH SUCH IGNORANCE!
THIS IS SASSY SISTER SANDA FROM THE SEVENTIES... WHEN BLAXPLOITATION WAS ALL THE RAGE, COMICS CAPITALISED! HOWEVER, THEY STILL RELIED ON RACIAL STEREOTYPES TO GET OVER THEIR NARRATIVE.
WHAT'S THE DRAMA MAMA? I WAS BORN ON A GAMBLING TABLE UNDERNEATH A BROTHEL. I FOUGHT CRIME SINCE I WAS NINE, STILL REPPING THE M-I-G-H-T-Y FINE!
WHAT THE FUDGE BRUV? THAT'S AN AWFUL ORIGIN STORY!
THIS IS THE MOST POPULAR VERSION OF YOU. THERE WASN'T MUCH IN THE CHARACTER DEVELOPMENT DEPARTMENT, BUT NINETIES SOLD A SHED-LOAD OF VARIANT COVERS!
F'RSOOTH, I LIKETH TO SQUARE GUYS WITH BIG GUNS 'R DISTAFF WITH BALLSY BAZOOKAS!
SERIOUSLY, LIKE HOW IS THAT TINY WAIST SUPPORTING THE TOP PART OF HER BODY? THAT, LIKE, DEFIES HASHTAG GRAVITY FAM.
AND WHY DOESN'T SHE HAVE FEET?

AND YOU ARE?

TIS TIMETH F'R US TO SMITETH F'R SOOTH, JUSTICE AND THE SOUTH LONDON WAY!

OF COURSE YOU'RE NOT IN SOME WEIRD WEBCOMIC. THIS IS ALL A DREAM. YOU'LL WAKE UP SOON. STILL WOULDN'T EXPLAIN THESE PARALLEL VERSIONS OF US APPEARING TOGETHER AT THE SAME POINT...

WELL, I AM 'DIVERSITY QUOTA SANDA'--MADE SOLELY FOR THE PURPOSE TO SHOW THAT COMIC BOOK PUBLISHERS CARE ABOUT REPRESENTATION AND NOT TOKENISM (TEE HEE).

NAH. NO WAY IS SOMEONE WRITING MY STORY. I'M NOT SUM CHEESY COMIC CHARACTER!

YOUR SMITE IS OUTTA SIGHT!

SHEESH! SO, LIKE, WHY ARE YOU ALL HERE THEN?

THE LEAGUE OF EXTRAORDINARY SANDAS HAVE FINALLY DUN SUM UNIVERSAL TRAVELLING, A$$ SMACKING CROSSOVER, TO SOLVE THE MYSTERY OF THOSE DAMN SMASH PLANTS!

WE ALL KNOW THAT THE BITES OF THE SMASH PLANTS CHANGE PEOPLE INTO PHYSICAL MANIFESTATIONS OF THEIR ANXIETIES AND FEARS.

YEAH, SO? I'VE FIGURED THAT, TOO.

BUT THERE IS SOMETHING ELSE. SOMETHING WE ALL ARE MISSING...

V'RILY, TOGETH'R, THE SANDAS CAN HAST'T THE KNOWLEDGE TO SAVETH OUR INDIVIDUAL REALITIES FROM THE SMASHETH PLANTS.
AND HOW DO YOU KNOW THAT?
ALRIGHT, CHILL. THIS TEAM-UP, CROSSOVER THING IS NONSENSE. LISTEN, THE SMASH PLANTS RELEASE CHEMICALS, VAPOURS, PORES, AND THIS CHANGES WHATEVER WORLD YOU'RE ON.
I DECODED DR. MALULEKE'S NOTES! I'VE GOT BARE MEDICAL KNOWLEDGE, FAM. SIMPLES.
OH OKAY. JOB DONE. WE'LL BE OFF THEN.
VERILY.
FO' SURE!
SERIOUSLY, IS THAT ALL YOU NEEDED?

YUP. LATERS! ALSO, THANKS! YOUR MEDICAL KNOWLEDGE JUST SAVED THE MULTIVERSE...
MY MEDICAL KNOWLEDGE?
IT COULDN'T SAVE YOU...
BUT IT'S NOT ME THAT NEEDS TO BE SAVED.

EWWW, LURKIES!

UGH! I PREFERRED IT WHEN YOU WERE IN THAT TRANCE THINGIE! YOU WERE IN SOME WALKING DEAD ZONE FOR LIKE 10 MINUTES. THAT SAID, WE GOT SOME STUFF SUSSED!
LIKE WHAT?

THEY TOLD ME THAT DR. MALULEKE'S THESIS WAS RIGHT! PLANET DIVOC'S INVOLVEMENT WITH PLANETS IN DISTRESS HAS LED TO SOME PROPA DISASTERS. IT WAS ADRO WHO FEARED HELPING SPECIES FROM DIFFERENT PLANETS WOULD EVENTUALLY BACKFIRE ON DIVOC-91. IT SURE DID DOE!
THEN THE BABY ALIENS FELL ILL WHEN HUMANS BEGAN TO ARRIVE AND THAT KINDA PROVED ADRO'S THEORY 'CORRECT' TO BASIL AND EVERYONE HERE, BUT REALLY, IT'S ADRO'S FEARS THAT WERE BROUGHT TO LIFE BY THE SMASH PLANTS.
YUP. WE TOTALLY SAID THAT.
FOR SURE, THOSE EXACT SAME WORDS.
SO JUST TO CLARIFY YOUR LONG EXPOSITION... ADRO'S FEARS ARE ACCIDENTALLY KILLING THE BABIES AND THEN BLAMING THAT ON US?
YUP! ALSO, NO PRESSURE, BUT THERE'S STILL SOME MASSIVE ASTEROID HEADING TOWARDS EARTH! WHAT ARE WE GOING TO DO?
WELL, WE ARE GOING TO DEAL WITH ADRO! WE'RE GONNA SMASH THE SMASH PLANTS! AND THEN DEAL WITH THE ASTEROID.
HOW?

WELL, FIRST OF ALL WE'RE GOING TO STAND IN A HEROIC POSE.
AND THEN?
WE'RE GOING TO WAIT FOR THE 'TO BE CONTINUED' SIGN!
TO BE CONTINUED!

CHAPTER 8:
REMEMBERING TO RETURN

Art & Colours: Rudy Loewe
Words: Phelisa Sikwata
Letters: Hassan Otsmane-Elhaou
Cover: Warwick Johnson-Cadwell

"BUYELA.KHUMBULA."
"RETURN. REMEMBER."
VAAPASEE. YAAD HAL

BREATHE,
STANDWA SAM.
BREATHE.
MALU...
MALULEKE...
DOCTOR!
WHERE
AM I?
I WAS TOLD YOU
CAME HERE TO
REMEMBER.

WE NEED ANSWERS!
THE "L" IN BASIL STANDS FOR LIARS!
WHERE'S THAT PIERCED WEIRDO YOU'RE ALWAYS WITH?
I JUST WANT TO GO HOME.
of Adve
Scientists for
Leadership in
ARAMINTA?!
SHE...SHE'S QUEUING FOR THE SUBSPACE RADIO.
BUT WE'RE ALL HERE.
rsity
GOOD HOMO SAPIENS, WE HAVE TAKEN ALL YOUR ASKS TO ACCOUNT.
AND OUR SILENCE IS NOT A RESULT OF FOUL PLAY. YOU CAN TRUST US...
AND ADRO IS--
WHERE IS ADRO?!
ARAMINTA! YOU'RE SCARING US!

moya moya moya moya
WHAT HAVE YOU FORGOTTEN?
UNDER ALL THAT HARD FEAR, WHAT HAVE YOU BURIED?
WHAT ABOUT YOU NEEDS YOU HERE, NOW?

A while later...

I HEAR YOU.
AND I LOVE YOU, MY CHILD.

MUM?
CAN YOU SEE ME?
MY CHAMPO, YOU'RE ALIVE! ARE YOU COMING BACK? SOME SAY YOUNG PEOPLE HAVE BEEN--
CHRKK ZT!
MORE CLEARLY THAN I EVER HAVE.
BZZZ ZT!
WHERE IS SANDA?
SHE'S TRYING TO FIND OUR WAY BACK HOME. SHE SENDS HER LOVE.
CLICK

IS SHE AWAKE?
NO, BUT SHE'S NO LONGER FIGHTING WHAT HAS TAKEN HER.

WHAT DOES THAT MEAN?
I DON'T KNOW.

YOU, LIKE EVERYONE ELSE, WERE BORN A PIECE OF THE KNOWING.
REMEMBER TO BREATHE IN UNISON.

IT IS TIME TO RETURN, BELOVED.

CHAPTER 9:
THE PLACE WHERE
WE STOP THE STORY
Story: Planet Divoc-91 Team
Art & Colours: James Devlin
Words: Sara Kenney
Letters: Hassan Otsmane-Elhaou
Cover: Alitha Martinez

IT'S TIME TO RETURN...
I'M OKAY.
TENDAI, THANKS FOR WATCHING OVER ME. YOU'RE A GOOD FRIEND.
I WAS WORRIED ABOUT YOU, WHERE WERE YOU?
TAKIN' TIME. WE NEED TO GET EVERYONE TOGETHER.

SURROUNDED BUT FEEL SO LONELY.
CAN'T TAKE THIS ANYMORE.
CAN'T STOP SNACKING.
PEOPLE DON'T LIKE ME.
Board of Adver... ...th (It's for Intergalactic Leadership... (ASIL)
I JUST DON'T LIKE PEOPLE!!
IT'S NOT FAIR.
IS IT WEIRD I LOVE QUARANTINE?
MAKE IT STOP!

WE'RE ALL BORN A PIECE OF THE KNOWING...

SO, A LOT OF YOU HEARD MY VIEWS DURING HARVEST DUTIES. I KNOW I'VE WITHDRAWN BUT I'VE BEEN THINKING AND NEED TO SHARE.

WE CAN'T STAY HERE, THIS PLACE IS TOXIC! I'M GONNA BE HONEST WITH YOU ALL. THE SMASH PLANTS ARE LITERALLY MAKING OUR WORST FEARS A REALITY.
WE HAVE TO RETURN TO EARTH, TOGETHER--
WHY WE GONNA TRUST YOU?

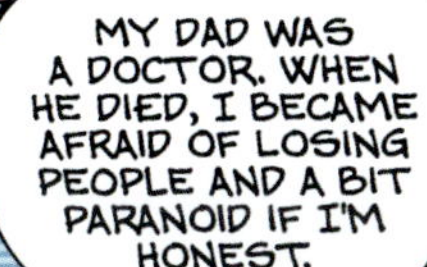

MY DAD WAS A DOCTOR. WHEN HE DIED, I BECAME AFRAID OF LOSING PEOPLE AND A BIT PARANOID IF I'M HONEST.
I'VE LEARNT FROM MY TIME HERE THAT AVOIDING UNCERTAINTY IS IMPOSSIBLE. IT'S IMPORTANT WE LEARN TO TOLERATE IT.
HOW WE SUPPOSED TO DO THAT?

SEPARATE OUT WHAT WE CAN CHANGE OR CONTROL FROM WHAT WE CAN'T.
FOCUS OUR ENERGIES ON SOLVABLE PROBLEMS.
WE NEED TO RETURN HOME, WITH OUR ALIEN FRIENDS, GET THE BABY ALIENS HEALTHY AGAIN... AND BEAT THIS ASTEROID.
SHE'S GOT A POINT.

WE'VE FOUND COMMUNITY HERE. WE MUSTN'T LET THOSE WITH FEAR AND HATRED IN THEIR HEARTS DIVIDE US.

Later...
I'M SORRY, SANDA. I HAVE SOMETHING TO TELL YOU.
WHAT'S UP, BUDDY?

REMEMBER I SAID CHAMPO WAS THE CHOSEN ONE? AND INVITED THEM TO THINK WITH US ON THE ASTEROID PLANS?

I LIED. THERE'S NO SUCH THING AS A CHOSEN ONE.

I SAID IT BECAUSE YOU HUMANS ARE GOOD AT FALLING INTO YOUR ALLOCATED ROLES. I FAILED TO RECOGNISE YOUR LEADERSHIP POTENTIAL.

IT'S AMAZING HOW FAR YOU'VE COME EVEN THOUGH NONE OF US BELIEVED IN YOU.
TENDAI!

CHAMPO AND I ARE DIFFERENT, BUT THAT'S WHY WE'RE A GOOD TEAM. I DON'T NEED ANYONE'S PERMISSION TO BE UNAPOLOGETICALLY ME.
ROARRRAARG!

THE VIRUS CAME FROM SPORES IN THAT TOILET PAPER.
IT'S GOT TEENY TINY SUCKERS SO IT CAN CLING TO PEOPLE'S FEET. THAT'S HOW IT SPREADS.

THE ONLY THING THAT SPREADS AROUND HERE ARE YOUR LIES ABOUT US INFECTING THE BABY ALIENS.

WE'RE GONNA ZAP THEM TO MARS, RIGHT?
TEMPTING.
ARAMINTA AND ADRO ARE VICTIMS TOO, SO THEY'RE COMING WITH US.
I'LL GET THEM TO THE HOSPITAL. YOU CALL HOME.

CHAMPO, YOUR INSIGHTS ABOUT ASTEROID TRAJECTORIES ARE BRILLIANT. THEY'VE CHANGED OUR THINKING.
YOUR UNIQUE PERSPECTIVE FROM PLANET DIVOC-91 IS INVALUABLE.
WE'RE READY TO COME HOME. TO HELP.

WE WANT TO WORK WITH YOU. BUT OTHERS WANT YOU TO STAY PUT.
GIVE US A FEW MORE MONTHS.

WE DON'T HAVE THAT TIME...

OKAY. WE'LL GET THEM TO LISTEN. YOU BE READY WITH YOUR PLANS.

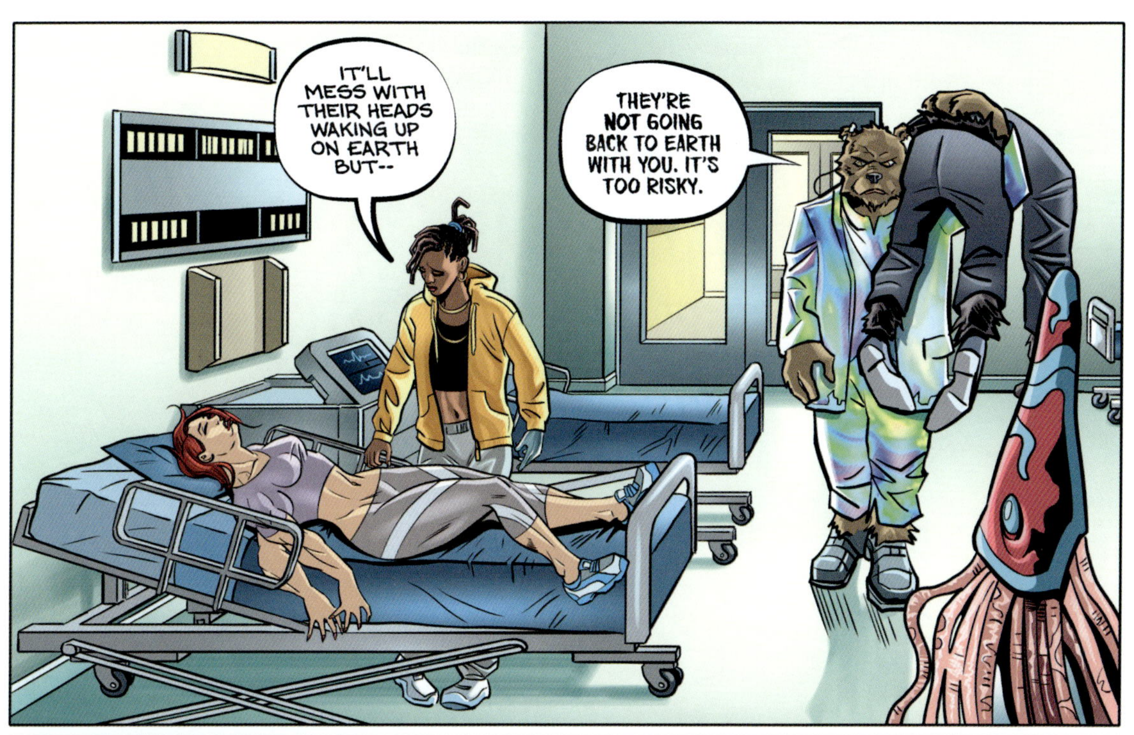

IT'LL MESS WITH THEIR HEADS WAKING UP ON EARTH BUT--
THEY'RE NOT GOING BACK TO EARTH WITH YOU. IT'S TOO RISKY.

ARAMINTA
ADRO
DR. MALULEKE'S NOTES SAID THAT AS SOON AS THEY'RE AWAY FROM THE SMASH PLANTS THEY'LL RECOVER.
IT'S A GAMBLE.

ALL MY WINS ARE BASED ON FAILURES. C'MON, IT'S A CALCULATED RISK.

THE SITUATION ON EARTH IS FRAGILE. HUMANS AND 'ALIENS', AS YOU CALL US, ARE COLLABORATING WELL, BUT IF THEY SEE THE STATE OF ARAMINTA...
HA! WE'RE USED TO CELEBS BECOMING WARPED MONSTERS.

ANYWAYS, NOBODY'S GONNA GIVE ARAMINTA A SECOND LOOK WHEN WE RETURN TO EARTH WITH THESE CUTIES!

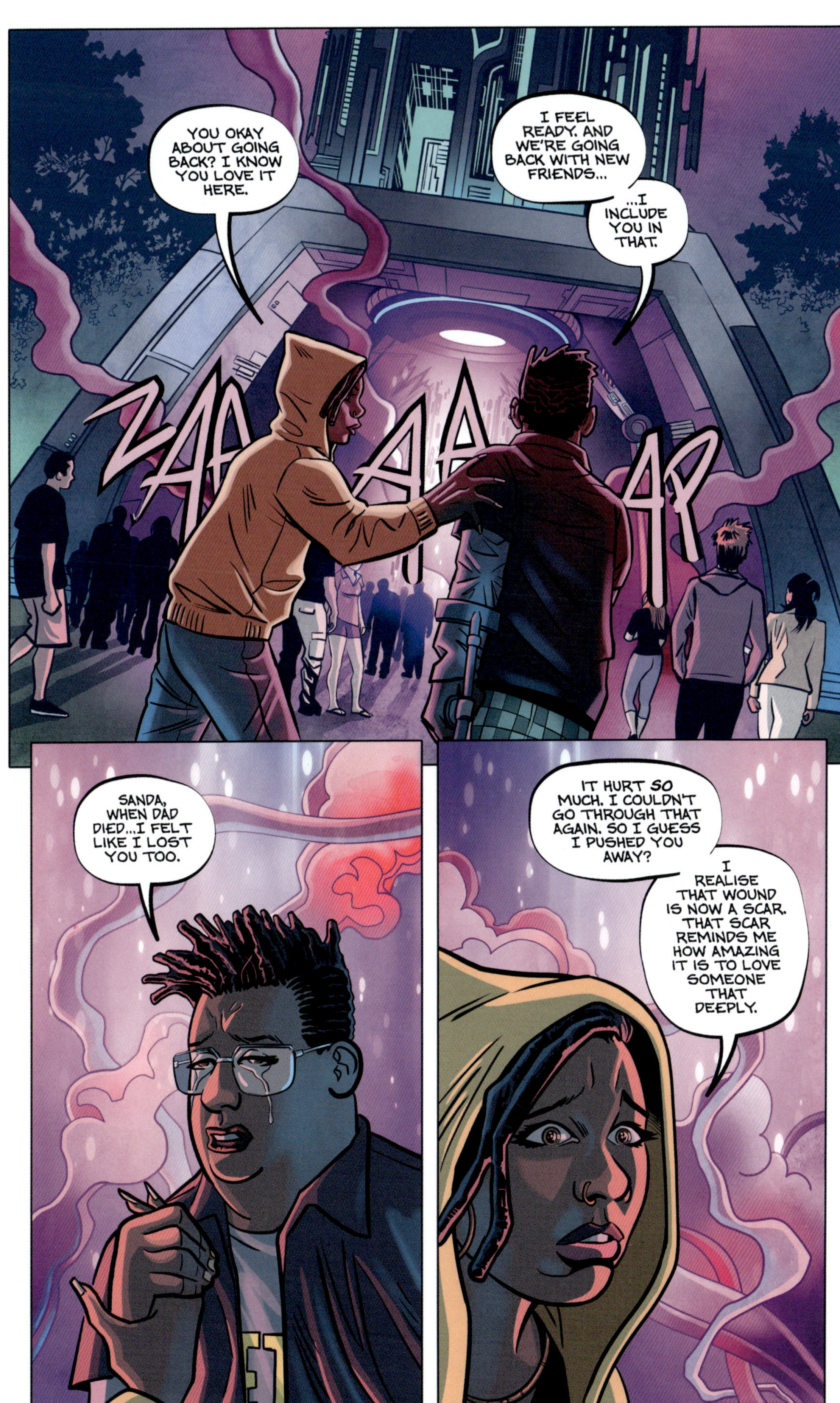

YOU OKAY ABOUT GOING BACK? I KNOW YOU LOVE IT HERE.
I FEEL READY. AND WE'RE GOING BACK WITH NEW FRIENDS...
...I INCLUDE YOU IN THAT.
ZAP
ZAP
ZAP
SANDA, WHEN DAD DIED...I FELT LIKE I LOST YOU TOO.
IT HURT SO MUCH. I COULDN'T GO THROUGH THAT AGAIN. SO I GUESS I PUSHED YOU AWAY?
I REALISE THAT WOUND IS NOW A SCAR. THAT SCAR REMINDS ME HOW AMAZING IT IS TO LOVE SOMEONE THAT DEEPLY.

CHAMPO, YOU'VE ALWAYS BEEN THERE FOR ME, UNCONDITIONALLY. SO FROM NOW ON, WE TALK. NO WALLS.
IT'S TIME TO RETURN...
ZAAAP

EPILOGUE...

No 36772 Friday January 5 2024 £28.00
EVENING TIMES
FLORIDA DESTROYED BY BREAKOFF Page 4
WE'RE BACK WITH THE BLAH BLAH
WestEnders
BLAH BLAH
BLAH BLAH
BLAH BLAH
BLAH BLAH
PLUS
TV GUIDE
WITH KIRSTEN MURRAY
TERRY FOR AN OSCAR
PLUS
£13,000
JACKPOT
NEAR MISS
EXTINCTION LEVEL EVENT NO LONGER A THREAT IN EXTRAORDINARY INTERGALACTIC EFFORT TO DEFLECT ASTEROID
BY SARA KENNEY
HOROSCOPES WITH DEVLIN - PAGE 24

One year later...
WONDER HOW TENDAI AND BOBBIE ARE GETTING ON?
GUTTED THEY DIDN'T COME BACK WITH US!
DEVASTATED, BUT SOMEONE HAD TO CLEAR OUT THE SMASH PLANTS.

THAT PLANET'S BEEN A SAFE HAVEN FOR THOUSANDS OF YEARS. THEY NEEDED TO MAKE IT RIGHT.

KIDDOS. EARS MUST HAVE BEEN BURNING...ARE THEY EVEN EARS? ANYWAY, CALL FOR YOU.

WE KNOW YOU'RE JUST GETTING OVER THE ASTEROID. BUT...
WITH THE SMASH PLANTS GONE, YOU'LL LOVE WHAT WE'VE DONE WITH THE PLACE.

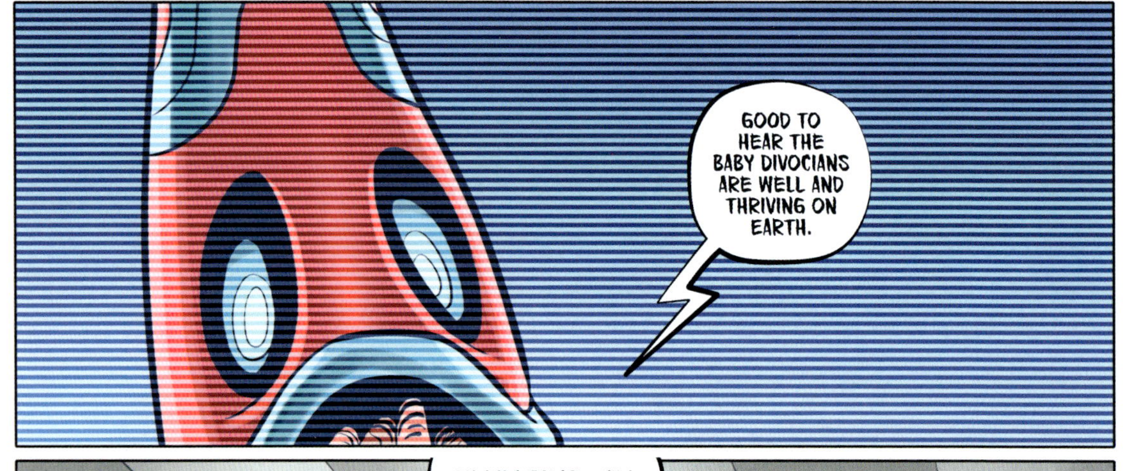

GOOD TO HEAR THE BABY DIVOCIANS ARE WELL AND THRIVING ON EARTH.

OH MY DAYS, WILL YOU JUST SPILL IT. WHAT'S UP?
THE MALUM. THEY ATTACKED MARS. WE NEED TO GET THE YOUNG MARTIANS TO DIVOC-91.

HOLD UP. THERE ARE MARTIANS?!

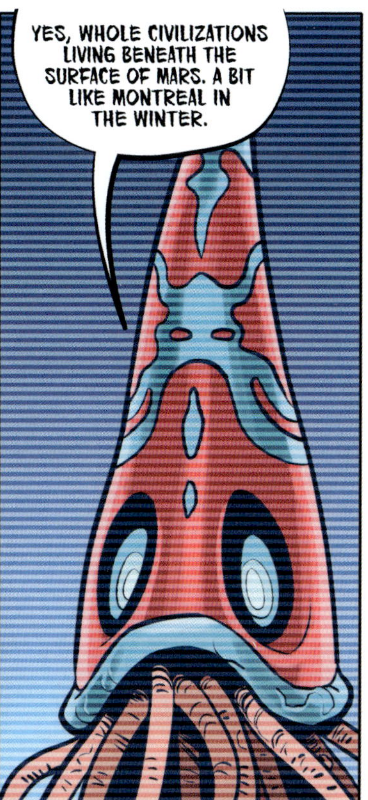

YES, WHOLE CIVILIZATIONS LIVING BENEATH THE SURFACE OF MARS. A BIT LIKE MONTREAL IN THE WINTER.

HOW COULD WE NOT KNOW THIS?

DO YOU NEED A LIST OF ALL THE THINGS HUMANS HAVE ONLY JUST 'DISCOVERED'.
THAT SAID, WE NEED YOUR IDEAS AND WISDOM, WELL CHAMPO'S, AND YOUR LEADERSHIP! SO YOU'LL COME?

YES!!!
ONCE A DIVOCIAN, ALWAYS A DIVOCIAN... WE'RE READY THIS TIME.
ZAP AWAY!
THE END!

SOUNDTRACKING PLANET DIVOC-91 BY JOE MUGGS

When I was asked to get involved with Planet Divoc-91, I was already immersed in thought about how the pandemic was affecting music cultures and subcultures. It was inevitable I would be: for 20-plus years it's been my job to chart and document subcultures. But as Covid hit the UK in March 2020, my attention to scenes and their evolution was extra focused for a couple of reasons.

First, my book *Bass, Mids, Tops: An Oral History of Soundsystem Culture* had just been published at the end of 2019. It traced the ripples that spread out from the arrival of Caribbean soundsystems and reggae basslines in the UK over five decades. Compiling, writing and promoting it had opened my eyes to how the most minute of personal interactions can be the transmitters of vast and vital historical currents. I should have been out promoting the book through 2020, but for obvious reasons ended up stuck at home with a head full of thoughts on the topic.

The second thing was the death of the great Andrew Weatherall. I had been a fan of the DJ, producer, artist and storyteller since I was 15, and in recent years had got to know him and work with him. He died on February 17th, so the rest of that month I was writing obituaries, talking to mutual friends, and thinking a lot about his status as a great connector across scenes and subcultures. The last public event I attended before lockdown hit this country was as part of a panel discussion about his legacy at inner city electronic festival in Leeds on the 7th March.

All of this, then, made for a heady brew as the isolation of lockdown and fears for the very future of the music scenes I'd been connected to for so long forced big questions to bubble up in my mind about what it all meant and where it was all going. My creative friends were losing their livelihoods, there was talk of mass venue bankruptcies and even the end of music scenes full stop as it seemed possible a whole generation might miss their first experiences of shows and festivals. As the crisis went on, old certainties about culture and counterculture were turned on their head as rebellion in the shape of 'plague raves' and vaccine denial became associated with the worst of reactionary views.

So the opportunity to recruit musicians and DJs from the UK, India and South Africa to be part of Planet Divoc-91 was a fantastic one. Not only did their mixes and live sets add a new dimension to the story itself, but we got to weave their evolving experiences into the stories and research we were getting from the young people working on the project. Discussing the pandemic, the reaction of scenes to it, how information is transmitted among people who might be removed from or suspicious of mainstream media: all of this helped paint a bigger and clearer picture of what was happening around us.

We didn't find easy answers to anything, but we weren't looking for them. Just as when Divoc-91 participants interviewed government representatives and medics, it was about opening up conversations and lines of communications across continents, scenes and social divides. And that is as vital as ever: of course with Covid's continuing impact – not to mention wars, financial crises and the climate emergency – existential threats remain painfully obvious to people and cultures. But what we have learned without question in the past two years is just how much we all value our cultures in times of crisis.

And, though it may not be so obvious in what we're constantly reminded is a post-truth era, how vital those cultures and shared interests can be for spreading truth and impetus to positive action. The modern age may have made the forces of misinformation, inequality and hate seem overwhelming at many points. But it has also shown us how even our smallest and most seemingly inconsequential actions and choices – in listening, talking, sharing and dancing – can have lasting and major value in fighting those forces.

GRANDMIXXER

- Introduce yourself! Who are you, where are you from and how would you describe what you do artistically/musically to someone unfamiliar with your kind of music?

My name is GRANDMIXXER and I am from Kennington, South London. I am a DJ / producer with intergalactic skills trying to raise my music sound/scene from an underground state to a worldwide movement that all can enjoy.

- Tell us about the mix you did for Divoc-91: how did you approach it and does it represent what you usually play?

100% my musical truth at the time of recording, loads of my own tunes plus bits that I was dropping on my Rinse and NTS's show.

- Sorry if this one is painful, but how has the Covid crisis impacted your work and the scene(s) you operate in?

Since the onset of lockdown, I have recorded 95% of the radio that I do from home, which has been an experience and has helped me stay sharp and motivated while we were all in our houses.

- How about misinformation about Covid and vaccines? Has that been a problem in music scenes and around where you live?

To be honest, I tried my hardest to stay away from asking people about their stances on vaccines and such as it can lead to arguments and contention with those around you who may be misinformed and making a choice or choices that you personally wouldn't. I will say there are many great fact-checking sources out there for people who want real scientific and empirical information on any given subject.

- On the flip side of that: have you seen any good examples of people and scenes spreading good information and positive messages?

There is a balance: it's all about where you are looking. I have seen a big push towards better health in general be it mental or physical and that can only be a good thing.

- How much has the crisis of the past couple of years changed how you feel about mass communication? Do you see any reasons to be hopeful we might be able to change social media and cultural networks for the better?

Mob rule reigns and always has reigned supreme in any society. The way we speak to each other online is a reflection of how we feel about ourselves, There are few rules in the virtual world and it is interesting to see how we will use social media in the future. I am a perpetual optimist so I will always hope for the best.

LCY

– Introduce yourself! Who are you, where are you from and how would you describe what you do artistically/musically to someone unfamiliar with your kind of music?

I am LCY and I would describe myself as a producer, artist and label owner.

– Tell us about the mix you did for Divoc-91: how did you approach it and does it represent what you usually play?

I really enjoyed putting my mind to creating the mix for Divoc-91. I tried my best to think about what it would look like and the type of story it would accompany and curated the mix according to that.

– Sorry if this one is painful, but how has the Covid crisis impacted your work and the scene(s) you operate in?

Mentally and financially it took a toll, but I definitely have had enough space to realize my blessings within this time as I think a bad mind space can often make your thoughts very centred around self… I now feel grateful that my time wasn't as bad as it could have been and that I made it through to the other side both times.

– How about misinformation about Covid and vaccines? Has that been a problem in music scenes and around where you live?

I think en masse it is a problem. I think a lot of my peers are of the age where their choices around the vaccine thankfully don't affect their mortality – though the loved ones that did live with high-risk people all knew to research. And my mum who works as nursing staff has seen a very real side of the effects and lack of vaccines.

– On the flip side of that: have you seen any good examples of people and scenes spreading good information and positive messages?

I can't think of any of the top my head other than this one. I also really loved Dolly Parton's Vaccine / Jolene cover and work.

– How much has the crisis of the past couple of years changed how you feel about mass communication? Do you see any reasons to be hopeful we might be able to change social media and cultural networks for the better?

I think of course it all links back to data laws needing to change to protect the people that use the internet from being pawns, whether it's regarding personal or capital gain, it's an incredibly scary thing to imagine yourself succumbing to misinformation but it happens every day. I would really honestly love to shoot mark Zuckerberg out into space with the rest of the Facebook / Meta servers. I am still hopeful but I think it would take radical mass action against capitalism and boycotting to extinct both of them, which I could firmly get behind.

JUICE ALEEM

- Introduce yourself! Who are you, where are you from and how would you describe what you do artistically/musically to someone unfamiliar with your kind of music?

Hey. My name is Juice Aleem. I'm an artist from Birmingham UK and I am a musician who mostly works in the hip hop movement, and to this end, I also co-direct a few festivals such as High Vis and B-Side hip hop festival in the Midlands. I also write and present workshops dealing with a mix of education, art and Afrofuturism under the name Afroflux.

- Tell us about the mix you did for Divoc-91: how did you approach it and does it represent what you usually play?

The playlist was a version of me presented for people like me. The combination of comic and hip hop cultures is something I've been about for a long time and even make space for in a few of the events I help put together. I don't DJ much for the public these days but this playlist is a touch of how I get down.

- Sorry if this one is painful, but how has the Covid crisis impacted your work and the scene(s) you operate in?

A lot of reflection, loss, and lots of reminders to stay human in this world.

- How about misinformation about Covid and vaccines? Has that been a problem in music scenes and around where you live?

I'm not sure if any of this has been an issue other than from a governmental level. Leading a country by waiting to react to what's being said on social media has helped no one.

- On the flip side of that: have you seen any good examples of people and scenes spreading good information and positive messages?

The humans who have understood that hygiene, space, allowance and health must always be considered when putting on events and dealing with the people.

- How much has the crisis of the past couple of years changed how you feel about mass communication? Do you see any reasons to be hopeful we might be able to change social media and cultural networks for the better?

That's a pretty loaded question but I will say that we can finally get to the level where we actually have a media that is social.

Check out Juice Aleem's mix at:
youtube.com/watch?v=xy4E4XVgbzo

IFEOLUWA

- Introduce yourself! Who are you, where are you from and how would you describe what you do artistically/musically to someone unfamiliar with your kind of music?

I'm Yewande, aka Ifeoluwa, and I'm from London, born in Belgium and with Nigerian heritage. I'm a multidisciplinary artist, writer, academic and DJ. I play both high energy global club music and experimental fringe sounds – basically anything that sounds weird that I can dance to.

- Tell us about the mix you did for Divoc-91: how did you approach it and does it represent what you usually play?

It was a weird time for me. I'd ended up moving around a lot in the pandemic with unstable housing. Like most people, I faced uncertainty with gigs, employment and just general doom, so I did what I always do in these situations: I chose the songs that got me through those times. Sounds I immersed myself in to escape, to feel, to connect. That's why it isn't just new music, there are tracks that inspired me and a few I enjoyed dancing around my room to during lockdown.

- Sorry if this one is painful, but how has the Covid crisis impacted your work and the scene(s) you operate in?

I've had Covid twice now. The first time I ended up in the hospital and that sent everything up in the air. I went from working at 100 miles per hour to being unable to walk and hardly breathe. I faced a lot of nastiness during this period and saw the worst of people in my 'scene'. A painful reminder that a scene is just that and not a community. It was near impossible to work for months and months. I nearly gave up and while everyone went headfirst into hypercapitalism, myself and a few others took a step back. This is the bit of the scene I'm part of and where I've found solace: with those who put people first.

- How about misinformation about Covid and vaccines? Has that been a problem in music scenes and around where you live?

Not so much, but general British colonial hedonism has led to a very lax attitude with a disregard for anyone else – especially disabled people.

- On the flip side of that: have you seen any good examples of people and scenes spreading good information and positive messages?

For sure! Not to fall into trap of toxic positivity, of course, but I guess all the people who continued to share their art during their darkest days and who still supported people no matter what. I don't want to name people in particular due to the sensitive situation around it, but a lot of marginalised people have shown there are better days to come even if we don't feel it now – and there are plenty more bangers too.

- How much has the crisis of the past couple of years changed how you feel about mass communication? Do you see any reasons to be hopeful we might be able to change social media and cultural networks for the better?

The amount of misinformation that spreads like wildfire will never not annoy me. I think people find comfort in joining whatever the general consensus is when it comes to something they're unfamiliar with. Most people can't sit with uncomfortable truths but a platform I was surprised to find directly challenges this is TikTok. There are so many information videos from those in various industries that have short videos on various geopolitical events, climate change, elections, the human body, how to bake, etc that is quick and easy to digest. I've also personally used social media to connect with other Black femmes and people in the music industry with similar views on how we can collectively enact change. Once you get older, it's harder to make friends, especially when you're Black but in one or two Tweets, you're connected with people just like you. It's a powerful tool but often misused.

Check out Ifeoluwa's mix at:
mixcloud.com/PlanetDivoc91/mix-by-ifeoluwa-chapter-4-its-just-a-phase

TOYA DELAZY

– Introduce yourself! Who are you, where are you from and how would you describe what you do artistically/musically to someone unfamiliar with your kind of music?

My name is Toya Delazy. I am South African born, living in East London. I am a live music producer, composer and rapper – I rap in my mother tongue Zulu over leftfield bass, techno, d'n'b and jungle beats in a genre I call Afrorave.

– Tell us about the mix you did for Divoc-91: how did you approach it and does it represent what you usually play?

The mix I did for Divoc-91 was experimental, literally. I learnt how to live produce and DJ during the lockdown and since all of our gigs got cancelled, the only way to "turn up the volume" was online, so I had to learn how to perform from home. I enjoyed live producing so much, it helped me channel all the pent up emotions, and sounds that moved me to connect with my peeps, even though we were not in the same room. So my gqomrave mix represented the mental journey of trusting the process & looking for the light at the end of the tunnel.

– Sorry if this one is painful, but how has the Covid crisis impacted your work and the scene(s) you operate in?

It was scary, and I lost a lot of money; entire campaigns that were set dissolved, and there was no backing in sight that I qualified for, from the government or any other music aid, so I really was on my own. Many of us were. So I decided to pour myself into music and made a new album, Afrorave Vol.1, and learnt how to live produce.

– How about misinformation about Covid and vaccines? Has that been a problem in music scenes and around where you live?

Yes, I fell into some of the rabbit holes. All I wanted to know was how to take care. Instead, the pandemic became extremely political, and divisive. As a South African, I've heard about weird inoculation campaigns by the likes of Wouter Basson during Apartheid (he's a cardiologist and former head of the country's chemical and biological warfare project, Project Coast), so I'm always apprehensive. In the music scene, most of the people around me take care so it hasn't affected me too much.

– On the flip side of that: have you seen any good examples of people and scenes spreading good information and positive messages?

I attended the 'Save Our Scene' march, where the dance community came together to uplift during this crisis. It was empowering to see everyone come together to keep the scene alive. That's what we do music for, sticking together even when it's tough.

– How much has the crisis of the past couple of years changed how you feel about mass communication? Do you see any reasons to be hopeful we might be able to change social media and cultural networks for the better?

As someone who has experienced both the highs and lows of socials, I wonder if we can change from 'performative wokeness' to true dialogue. Everyone has something to say and will do anything to be heard, even if it's breaking another person down for a laugh. This is the culture we live in and it's permeated into society, as we saw at the Travis Scott concert in the USA: while attendees were dying in the ambulances after the crowd surge, fans jumped on top of police vans for clout on Instagram. We have to have boundaries online, and common sense, and avoid going too far. As much as I do believe everyone has a right to say something, I don't believe we have to tolerate it if is harmful and doesn't resonate with our own experience – this is the root of poor mental health. The messaging the media sends us today still strips us of our own identity to commodify our experience for profit. I would like to see inclusivity that is more robust and less performative. It's nice to see hate messages and gross misinformation being filtered and taken down – that is a step in the right direction.

NV FUNK

- Introduce yourself! Who are you, where are you from and how would you describe what you do artistically/musically to someone unfamiliar with your kind of music?

NV Funk – performing artist based in Cape Town, South Africa. I produce and perform a South African created genre called Gqom. My unique art is DJing and playing live drums.

- Tell us about the mix you did for Divoc-91: how did you approach it and does it represent what you usually play?

I played my own music, so the approach was simple but effective: "Yes, this is the genre of music I perform!"

- Sorry if this one is painful, but how has the Covid crisis impacted your work and the scene(s) you operate in?

Covid-19 has completely shut down my industry for two years. So it's been really tough but also, I personally took so much from it. I had to drive my creative juice to my different business ventures. But I'm grateful for the experience and tough person Covid-19 has made me.

- How about misinformation about Covid and vaccines? Has that been a problem in music scenes and around where you live?

Not actually. I took the vaccine because I travelled for international gigs, so I had to get it.

- On the flip side of that: have you seen any good examples of people and scenes spreading good information and positive messages?

Yes, always. I'm surrounded by highly driven and positive people. So I don't need to look far for positivity.

- How much has the crisis of the past couple of years changed how you feel about mass communication? Do you see any reasons to be hopeful we might be able to change social media and cultural networks for the better?

Social media is at its forefront right now and everyone should use it to its advantage. We can launch businesses on platforms for free, and push it regardless of educational documents. So social media is a blessing to anyone at this stage in life.

Check out NV Funk's mix at:
mixcloud.com/PlanetDivoc91/mix-by-nv-funk-chapter-6-same-but-different

ANGEL-HO

- Introduce yourself! Who are you, where are you from and how would you describe what you do artistically/musically to someone unfamiliar with your kind of music?

I uncover queer ideologies throughout time and history by inverting them into classical art history or in period to contemporary music to recall ideologies of sexuality and gender identity.

- Tell us about the mix you did for Divoc-91: how did you approach it and does it represent what you usually play?

It represented what tastes I like, NYC being a huge inspiration and the works of Venus X and her impact. As for now, I am still very inspired by this and I now play hybrids of electronic music that are cross-genre.

- Sorry if this one is painful, but how has the Covid crisis impacted your work and the scene(s) you operate in?

It has taken everything away from me. I have been nearly homeless twice and received no support from the South African government. The scene is still thriving as younger DJs who came after me still operate as the DJs. However, I have been placed in their consciousness as someone who does not need to be regularly booked and this has led me to want to leave South Africa because I am a black sheep of the music industry here.

- How about misinformation about Covid and vaccines? Has that been a problem in music scenes and around where you live?

Yes, people are superstitious and sceptical. I believe you should get vaxxed.

- On the flip side of that: have you seen any good examples of people and scenes spreading good information and positive messages?

Not really. Everyone's self-centred around being 'hot' or someone of the moment. I'm out of touch when it comes to South Africa's localness because I am a citizen of the world, not South Africa alone. As a country with a legacy of corruption still happening today, I am proud to be unified with people on the African continent and from all over the world. My viewpoint is global, not a singular space.

- How much has the crisis of the past couple of years changed how you feel about mass communication? Do you see any reasons to be hopeful we might be able to change social media and cultural networks for the better?

Well, I am against the metaverse because they are training us to become their products and suppliers of their income. I am not playing by social media's rules. It's very dystopian. It made people more accustomed to feeling depressed if they do not match people's popular posts on social media, the endorphin rush received when scrolling has made me dependent on this rush, I now feel a need to distance myself from social media, it has messed up my business. I will one day sue Facebook for including an algorithm and ruining my livelihood. It all creates immense pressure to be successful when there is a system that is against you.

Check out Angel-Ho's mix at:
mixcloud.com/PlanetDivoc91/mix-by-angel-ho-chapter-7-crisis-of-existential-selves

ARJUN VAGALE

- Introduce yourself! Who are you, where are you from and how would you describe what you do artistically/musically to someone unfamiliar with your kind of music?

Hi, my name is Arjun Vagale. I'm primarily a DJ and producer based between Delhi and Goa, India. I've been in the business for about 25 years now. I also run a couple of record labels, a talent management agency, music school and have my hand in pretty much anything and everything to do with electronic music in India.

- Tell us about the mix you did for Divoc-91: how did you approach it and does it represent what you usually play?

The mix for Divoc-91 was made during the peak of the pandemic when we were all stuck at home and I was itching to play – so it's an all-out, banging, in-your-face mix of tracks that were doing it for me at the time. It does represent, to some degree, what I would play at the peak of my sets.

- Sorry if this one is painful, but how has the Covid crisis impacted your work and the scene(s) you operate in?

Naturally, everything came to a complete standstill and it affected everyone in the business – right from the DJs to club owners, bar staff and back end team like managers and agents. We had to close down our music school and let go of everyone. It was a heartbreaking situation that completely wiped out most independent businesses related to music and entertainment. To add to that, India had one of the worst second waves that crushed the health care system, and pretty much everyone I know knew someone who lost a family member or a friend. For a lot of younger artists that were just starting out or taking their first steps, they had to find alternative paths as the future of nightlife was uncertain… They didn't know if we would ever get back to normal.

- How about misinformation about Covid and vaccines? Has that been a problem in music scenes and around where you live?

To be honest, we were completely clueless! Information was scarce with little help coming from the media – often contradicting what the government was saying. Every healthcare professional had a different view, so it was hard to navigate what protocols one needs to set up. We didn't know how or when this would end, or how we would start to rebuild – it was a series of social experiments we needed to do, for ourselves, to figure out what works and wouldn't. We built our own standards and norms looking at what was happening worldwide.

- On the flip side of that: have you seen any good examples of people and scenes spreading good information and positive messages?

Now that we are slowly coming back to life, in hindsight, there has been some good that has come out of this – a lot more unity within the scene. People are looking out for each other, talking more, discussing strategies and generally helping each other so we can all come out of this stronger and wiser. We put out a charity compilation called SOS at the onset of the second wave, and I was amazed to see how united the dance music community was!

- How much has the crisis of the past couple of years changed how you feel about mass communication? Do you see any reasons to be hopeful we might be able to change social media and cultural networks for the better?

To be brutally honest, no! Social media is partly responsible for the heightened levels of stress and anxiety a lot of us are feeling. The world is now closer and connected like never before… but you look at the physical world around you, locally and culturally, we are all so different. What applies to someone on the other side of the world will be very different to my experience. Yet we will always be forced to compare ourselves no matter what. That's the bigger problem. I feel there is still much more to be learnt.

Three of the project leads discuss their own venture into the heart of Planet Divoc-91 amid the coronavirus pandemic.

CENTRE STAGE *by Bella Starling*

"Who should I trust?" comes a cry from the auditorium; a question I'm often asked as I stand on the stage of science communication.

"Scientists!"
"Oh, no you shouldn't!"

Truth is, of course, it depends.

Intelligent trust directs trust and mistrust according to the pillars of reliability, competence, and honesty (so says the formidable philosopher Onora O'Neill). Science is, by its nature, uncertain and sceptical with debate at its core. This can cause us to question its reliability. Scientists are humans, complete with political and social attitudes and motivations. But when, in early February 2020, I return from a work trip to Thailand, it's the scientific commentators and colleagues that I listen to and – against the government advice of the time – I self-isolate. Now, when I don my face mask, it's because I trust the weight of scientific evidence, even if this is still evolving.

"But how can I connect people to my science, engage them with my research?" comes another voice.

Start by earning trust, admitting to vulnerability, and not talking down to people. Then let creativity enter the spotlight. I couldn't do this part of my job without the creative partners I work with; together we inform, entertain, and open dialogue and meaning beyond the theatre of numbers integral to science. And this is part of what we aim to do with Planet Divoc-91. Science is part of culture, as culture is part of science.

This connection, this trust, has to be a two-way street. Covid-19 has laid bare the deep inequalities of our world. Science is not neutral or unprejudiced: racist hypotheses, a workforce that is not diverse, and discriminatory recruitment to research studies all exist. If I've learned one thing during the start of this project, it's the passion young people have for a more just world, more equity in science and society.

To achieve this desired equity, science must start listening to people's experiences and incorporating those into its practice. Making science and policy listen is also something we hoped to achieve with Planet Divoc-91 by feeding in the perspectives of young creators and readers to our august institutions.

"Has the role of science advice in government decision-making been clear during Covid?"

Many scientists are adamant that their role is to advise; government is the decision-maker. But government's insistence of "being led by the science" has been a common refrain. Sure, science can legitimise decision-making, but this narrative also has the potential to scapegoat scientists, turning them into the villains of the piece. Where then for science and public trust?

As stages across the globe plunge into a depressing darkness, I am joined onstage by my son. Like other young people, his world has been turned upside down, his future is less certain. It's my hope that Planet Divoc-91 will bring some light into this darkness, a way of engaging with the complexity of this pandemic and enabling young voices to influence science and policy. It's amazing to see its characters take to the global stage!

REIMAGINE AND REBUILD *by Nabeel Petersen*

I am one of the co-directors of the Pivot Collective: an NPO interested in egalitarian and collaborative knowledge production. In late 2019, we began working on a project with young adults in Cape Town called Young & Curious. It's a space to challenge themselves and others to explore, deconstruct and dismantle mental health; dare research and art to be more inclusive; spark conversations amongst young people, adult professionals and institutions; question dominant practices; and to be Young & Curious in any and all ways.

We should perhaps mention that South Africa remains segregated and unequal by the imagination of race, social status, gender, disability, age, etc. The legacy of Apartheid is a fire-breathing dragon bent on destruction, imposition and accumulation of wealth by those in power. Ideals of participation and collaboration are often what stories are made of.

Our imaginations are not active because we are continuously condensed by our need for work, education, food, services, etc. Apartheid lives here, hidden by white privilege and an often-passive acceptance of cumulative wealth at the expense of a suffering country, like a structural broom sweeping any challenge to the status quo under the proverbial carpet that is South Africa. There is a structural desire to attract investment and protect the prosperous. This jades our ability to imagine and dream often because we are stuck in a 24-hour cycle to earn a measly living. Our structures limit us, but together we have already reimagined who we could be and what we could do with some resources and respect as active humans.

We are a joyful, welcoming, curious and creative people. The young and young-at-heart continue to protest and imagine a better future, fuelled by tech and a support structure beyond our national borders: all of you! Planet Divoc-91 is a collective dream we all share. As you turn each page, we are there with you! Our team of future-designers just got bigger, more exciting. The support we don't find in South Africa resonated with and was situated within this broader Planet Divoc-91 team, and hopefully with you.

This is also THE opportunity to reimagine social life to be more conscious of others, ourselves, our actions, and our role as custodians of Earth. No structures are absolute and void of reimagining. Spaces to interweave imaginations should lead us through and beyond the arcs of our unwritten future. We should start writing our futures, together. Planet Divoc-91 is one such fertile space which brings us all together for a superbly collaborative edu-taining yet creative experience. A story unfolding through our interaction with people across the world. A space where we can reimagine and challenge dominant perceptions of static social groups and identities, and disrupt systems of exclusion, hierarchy and pedagogy. A space to imagine, design, laugh and be together. Imagination and the freedom to dream are our first steps towards realising the futures we all deserve.

COLLABORATING TO IMAGINE A BETTER FUTURE
by Sarah Iqbal

I'll never forget the rush I'd get from grabbing copies of my favourite comics from the musty book stalls at the railway station before jumping on a train. For most kids of my generation from the Indian middle-class, these low-cost comics were our travel companions, our window to illicit adventures which served as inspiration for our youthful exploits. From superheroes, dacoits and detectives to mythological gods and goddesses, stories in these modestly produced comics would educate and charge our imagination as we went about our secure lives. What's more, they were everywhere – at the barber shop, local grocery store, school libraries, and even at the roadside tea stalls.

Historically, India has had a strong tradition of storytelling. From oral storytelling through poetry and songs to dance theatre and scroll paintings of patua and pattachitra – artists would travel from village to village with their performances and scrolls, narrating stories of life and magical tales. Some sermonised, some educated, and some simply entertained.

Art combined with storytelling is a powerful tool for engagement. We have used contemporary and traditional Indian folk art in various public engagement programs informed by larger conversations around pressing issues. These participatory spaces and art and science/health collaborations have shown us how even most sensitive and complicated topics can be made palatable and accessible through art. In addition to art being a medium of participatory communication, as revolutionary history will tell us, it's an important medium for change, for a meaningful commentary of our times.

Among major fallouts, Covid-19 has exacerbated challenges faced by young people by putting their social and professional lives on hold. The uncertainty about the future punctuated by the pandemic and the imminent economic slump are diminishing their chances of a bright future. This is particularly worrying for India, a country that has world's largest youth demographic with more than 50% of its population under 25. Demography is an important measure of a country's growth and development, and India can only reap this demographic dividend by investing in young people and addressing their needs and rights. Just like their problems, their voices have been marginalised during the pandemic. Planet Divoc-91 speaks directly to this issue in a fun yet profound way and that's why it appealed to me right away.

Young people are important agents for social change; they are the future, but they are also the present. They need to be nurtured, empowered and heard in research and policy discourses that have bearing on their lives.

Several global problems that plague us today require global efforts and collaboration between different disciplines, institutions, and countries. Projects like Planet Divoc-91 provide a rich, unique platform for young people to appreciate diverse experiences and perspectives that would hopefully enable them to reflect upon and address these issues with empathy and a global sensibility.

These comics, we hope, will serve as an important chronicle of these times as seen and experienced by young people in different countries and their idea of a post-Covid world.

Here's to shaping a brighter future, together!

CAN UNDERSTANDING PUBLIC HEALTH DURING COVID-19 REVOLUTIONISE OUR FUTURE?

by Amber Naeem, age 16, UK

"Public health" is a term used often in the media — but what exactly does it mean? In an exclusive interview with the inspirational Professor Arpana Verma, we manage to get the lowdown on why public health is so important and how it can directly affect you.

In a blink of an eye, normalcy was brutally wrenched from our grasp, leaving many of us confused, anxious, and wondering what had caused our society to fall apart so easily. The stock market plunged to its lowest in 100 years, planes were instantly grounded, and schools were forced to shut abruptly one seemingly mundane Friday afternoon. I remember eagerly watching the TV that day, excited that I wouldn't have to go to school for the foreseeable future (not that the future was foreseeable); but that was a happiness that has since been replaced with fear and sadness at the reality of how the situation has affected my family and country.

Recently, I was given the opportunity to interview Professor Arpana Verma. The head of the Division of Population Health, Health Services Research and Primary Care, a World Health Organisation expert, and the director of Manchester Urban Collaboration on Health (MUCH), Professor Verma is one of the world's leading public health specialists. As a group of young people keen for knowledge to empower our own decisions, we were curious to know more about what public health actually is, how it influences the government's decisions, and what it means for the development of society.

WHAT IS PUBLIC HEALTH?

With an engaging and welcoming smile, Professor Verma first enlightened us as to what the often "difficult to define" public health sector means for us. "I'm obviously very biased," she remarked before launching into her explanation. Public health, she said, effectively combines the science and art of clinical practice — i.e. how doctors actually treat us as individuals — together with the protection of the population, health promotion, and examination of behaviour change. It not only looks at how these factors affect the health of individuals, but at how the UK can adapt its healthcare and social care services to improve the population health as a whole.

The role of public health studies during the pandemic has been monumental. With the combined expertise of all universities, the NHS, and local authorities, the public health sector has come together during the Covid crisis to work with ordinary people to assess the impact on communities and how this can be mitigated in the future. While some of their current research has involved looking at infection prevention and control, they are also investigating how the environment — particularly the social and economic disparities in society — may influence how different communities are affected. Throughout Professor Verma's explanation, there was a huge appreciation of the teamwork and the solidarity behind her workforce, which is something we can perhaps take away and echo through our own daily actions.

"You need both the quantitative and qualitative" was a phrase often repeated; that is, you need both data and real-world individual stories. This highlighted the importance of patient and public engagement in research to really understand population health and the factors that may influence it. There's an intricate balance between the two and because of this, public health acts as a bridge between the politics and economics of the government and the statistics of the science advisory committee.

"THIS IS AN OPPORTUNITY FOR REAL CHANGE."

"We are facing the biggest public health emergency of all time," Professor Verma said.

The global pandemic and its impact on the UK has brought our health inequalities into sharp focus. While the greatest risk factor has shown to be age, there is a much larger risk for those living in socioeconomically deprived areas and of BAME ethnic origin.

This begs the question: *why?* And, just as importantly, what can we do about it? In June 2020, it was found that people of BAME backgrounds had between a 10% and 50% higher risk of death when compared to white British backgrounds. However, there's a difference between merely mentioning the statistics and doing something to actively change them.

The pandemic has exposed the harsh realities of social inequalities in the UK, yet it has also given us a platform to vocalise our concerns and hopefully make a real difference. It has allowed us to focus on the politics of the situation and we must seize the opportunity, no matter our age or ethnicity, to address this situation.

Steps that all of us as members of public can take to make a change include:

1. Vote and understand what government manifestos and politicians are truly talking about.
2. Talk to politicians about their views. It is fundamental that young people feel empowered to do this, so contact your local MP and use the media to make a difference, especially for the people who don't have a voice.

We went into this interview expecting to learn about public health in the abstract, but we came away with a sense of how we too are part of it and even more importantly, how we can affect it. We can help make a difference. YOU can make a difference.

MAGNIFYING THE LEFT OUT SECTIONS IN THE PANDEMIC

by Swakshadip Sarkar and Vishwadeep Mane (age 25, India)

We started the year 2020 with great aspirations, completely unaware about what the year had in store for us. As the year progressed, we came to know about Covid-19 spreading in different parts of the world. On 22 March 2022, India went on a nationwide lockdown which left most of us locked in our homes. For many people, it was an exciting idea to be at home and not go to classes or work. People tried learning new things and pursued hobbies that they hadn't been able to do until now due to their workload. It was a struggle for many, too. Many people went jobless all over the world and many businesses went bankrupt. The pandemic made us realise that viruses are much stronger and more intelligent than human beings. However, when we talk about the hardships faced by people, we often forget a section of society who are otherwise neglected, even in normal conditions, i.e. the transgender community.

In India, the total population of transgender persons is around 487,803 (the identification of transgender or third gender in official certificates came later in 2014 following a National Legal Services Authority, Government of India (NALSA) verdict) with a literacy rate of 46%, according to the 2011 Census, compared to 74% of the general population. The transgender community has been stigmatised, neglected, and abused by different sections of society. They are very often disowned by their families and forced to live in poverty. Many of them cannot even finish school due to bullying and harassment from their peers and even teachers. The lack of gender sensitisation even leads the teachers to bully transgender kids. Even if they finish schooling and go on to higher education, they do not have adequate facilities like accommodation or gender-neutral toilets which creates an additional hurdle for them. Many transgender people lack any form of identification such as an Aadhaar card (like a Social Security Number) or voter IDs, making it hard to gain constitutional rights. It is not easy for transgender people to rent accommodation as most of the letting agencies and landowners refuse them. As per a 2017 report by the National Human Rights Commission (NHRC), 79% of transgender people either live in rented rooms or share accommodation with others.

Many of them are forced into begging or sex work to make ends meet. According to the 2017 NHRC report, 52.06% of transgender people earn below ₹10,000 a month. Although the 2014 Supreme Court in NALSA verdict ruled that transgender individuals are also entitled to the same rights as others, societal barriers and a lack of knowledge about gender identities stand tall in the way of their success. The Transgender Protection Act 2019, which was passed after many attempts, does not do a lot for the transgender community. Almost all the definitions in the act are either redundant or profuse regarding the community issues. The chapter which prohibits discrimination lacks enforcing authority, remedial measures, and punitive measures. There isn't a single organised protocol in the act that guides the medical community on the healthcare of transgender people. The National Council for Transgender Persons proposed by the Act has no independence to carry out functions and has a mere representation of five persons from the transgender community. Any kind of violence, including sexual abuse, against people from the trans community is punishable by a maximum term of only two years. The Act was passed without any transgender representation in Parliament and therefore, it lacks essential input from the transgender community.

Now with the pandemic, few crore Indians have lost their jobs and while it is still easier for cisgender individuals to find employment, it is not so for transgender individuals. Even if they manage to find jobs, their mobility is restricted. One such example is from Kerala state of India, where twenty-three transgender people were recruited to work at various positions in Kochi Metro railway service. In the first week of their job, eight of the twenty-three, all trans women, quit. Employed in a variety of roles, from ticketing to housekeeping staff, which paid between ₹9,000-₹15,000 a month, most of them found it impossible to make ends meet, especially since landowners in the city charged them ₹400-₹600 a day for the most basic accommodation if they agreed to rent a place to them at all. Most of them had to go back to sex work or begging and their dreams to make a decent income were crushed.

During the pandemic, many transgender individuals who were working had to return to their family homes and face harassment and discrimination from their relatives. For 'Hijras' (a cultural identity under the transgender umbrella) who earn mostly from begging and performing in social functions, it is even worse. They have lost their livelihood opportunities which has resulted in a decline of their socioeconomic conditions and psychological state. Considering the current pandemic situation, Kerala Government has announced they will provide free ration kits to 1,000 transgender individuals and accommodation facilities to the community. However, this appreciable step may not be enough as only a small portion of the transgender community are covered under this initiative. In the recently announced relief package by Central Government for the distressed sections of the population, there was no mention of transgender people as beneficiaries in their propositions. Many of them, especially in cities, are slum-dwellers where social distancing is almost impossible.

Many transgender people in India are afraid of the healthcare system and the pandemic only makes it worse. The sexual health of transgender people is always at the forefront of discussions while other health issues aren't often thought of. But with the pandemic, even sexual health takes a backseat as the healthcare system is on the brink of a crisis responding to the emergency. This causes a problem mainly for those with a HIV positive status and need monthly doses of antiretroviral therapy (ART) drugs, but many don't have access to such medicines leaving them particularly vulnerable to Covid-19. Many hospitals in India do not have transgender wards, so patients are assigned wards based on their assigned sex leaving them vulnerable inside the hospitals as well. This makes them averse to going into hospitals and getting treated. Many who were going through gender reassignment surgeries had to stop their procedures due to the hospitals becoming containment zones which can have a negative impact on their health.

In conclusion, while the pandemic has hit all sections of the society, the gravity is not the same for everyone. Under normal conditions, the transgender community has been ignored, harassed, and discriminated against by society. They have never had equal access to education or employment like the cisgender population. During the pandemic, their conditions have worsened with little or no access to food, finances, or healthcare. While the economy is recovering, special impetus needs to be given to uplift the transgender community, not only from the government level but also from the societal level, otherwise the impact of this pandemic on this community will be everlasting.

EVEN MERRY-GO-ROUNDS

by Phelisa Sikwata (age 23, South Africa)

Above are photographs of merry-go-rounds; one taken in Mfuleni, which has a predominately black population, and the other in Kenilworth, predominately white, both in Cape Town, approximately 30km away from each other. The Mfuleni merry-go-round design is one I'm used to. Every person from the township knows it, have old scars or dents from flying from it in high speed, and some (whom I've never understood) love being on it. Seeing the Kenilworth one, for the first and only time, wrapped me up in the bitterness that is the political and classist aftermaths that is clouding Cape Town.

In my earliest memories of being on a merry-go-round, I was instructed to hold on for dear life and I always instruct my younger sibling to do the same. Now odd years later, one taxi ride away, I was witnessing a miracle. This merry-go-round had seats, a chain to buckle up like, if you wished, a child could lift their arms up at high speed and feel the wind dance with their fingers without hesitation. But why hasn't this design reached my side of town? What is it about children where I'm from that is seemingly undeserving of such consideration?

Yes, it could be argued that parks are vandalised in the townships; I'm not oblivious to that fact and the chains probably wouldn't last a month. But with that said, the reasons behind this difference are the results of undermined equity.

Now my favourite folks are those oblivious to the links I'm referring to. Let's use pop culture. The music video for Harry Styles' Watermelon Sugar, for example. That video is sexy with people living their best lives at the beach, eating watermelon. In one random frame, with people loungingly performing for the camera, there's one person of colour walking around with a metal detector in the background; the undermining of historical symbolism of black and brown bodies near the ocean, and black and brown bodies doing minute, demeaning labour just for humour (in this instance, I can only assume the reasons for the frame). I am aware that it's a fun video with no malicious intent but when many parts of one's life are not basking in privilege, one can't help but find everything political. And by no means do I undermine the agency of the person of colour in the frame but share the ways we, as the human race, in our 'forgetting' and evolving, have made the mockery of black and people of colour palatable.

That even in one 'innocent' frame, with all the steps and people a video goes through before its release, there is a refusal to see and stop the little ways that perpetuates stigmas about race and class. Now that blind spot sits alongside that of the merry-go-rounds; that in the same city, the safety of black and brown children is not as considered as that of white children. This is not necessarily done deliberately either, but that absentmindedness is rooted in historical social constructs that deliberately undermine and dehumanize black lives.

The big, bad, emotionless -isms and structures, which thrive on excluding and marginalizing, influence the somewhat small things, like children of colour not having merry-go-rounds with chains to buckle up.

DEBUNKING THE MYTH AROUND MILITARY METAPHORS: WHY ILLNESS ISN'T A MATTER OF WINNERS AND LOSERS

by Katie Heyes, age 20, UK

Illustration by Hanna Gwynn

The militaristic approach to depicting sickness has quickly become a cliché of modern English vernacular. It is all too common in the media, particularly during the Covid-19 pandemic, that when discussing life-threatening illnesses, journalists tend to write something along the lines of someone who "lost" their battle with an illness or are "fighting" for their lives. American President Donald Trump further amplified these battle comparisons by describing himself as a "wartime president". However, what many of us don't realise is how inaccurate and potentially detrimental this language can be. This understanding is what we took away from our interview with Viral Immunologist, Dr Zania Stamataki.

When asked about the effectiveness of combat comparisons when describing severe illnesses like Covid-19 or cancer, Dr Stamataki was quick to point out that "a patient is never fighting a disease — the immune system is". In her opinion, the real "battle" is "humanity pitched against the virus".

Of course, there are good reasons people use these metaphors. War has likely become a common metaphor for a pandemic due to the sense of security and solidarity it provides to the public. These feelings are key to increasing morale when faced with such devastating illnesses. In this case, the spirit of camaraderie can be well founded. Recovering from a severe disease exhausts the body and the mind and can disrupt relationships with friends, family,

and even one's self-esteem. Thus, the image of "winning" such a mentally and physically draining battle may be appropriate for journalists wanting to highlight and embellish the immense bravery of patients.

However, whilst it's true that the immune system is working tirelessly to fight off a dangerous pathogen, Dr Stamataki continued to explain how it is completely "wrong" and "counter-intuitive" to use expressions such as "they've lost the battle with Covid-19" as it is not a "fight of equal terms". Employing terminology such as "losing the battle" with a disease can unintentionally imply that death is somehow a failure and that the virus is some sort of "winner". A statement like this not only undermines our understanding of how unpredictable and catastrophic these diseases are, but it inadvertently glorifies them as more powerful than the patient. Frequenting these metaphors can be extremely harmful as for someone with a terminal illness it could attach feelings of guilt and responsibility to the fact that their illness cannot be treated. The scary thing is that many of us simply don't realise what a dangerous precedent this sets as it's ingrained in common vocabulary.

Metaphors are indeed a powerful tool as a way to visualise and understand the world's dilemmas, but in terms of sensitivity, it would be wise for us to widen the language we use to prevent further amplifying problematic implications.

FIXING THE FRACTURE

by Vishwadeep Mane, age 25, India

We have been in an evolutionary arms race with the invisible and ubiquitous microbial world since the dawn of this Anthropocene age. To a few, climate change might seem like a hoax, but it is a peril that lingers all over our planet and the consequences of which are apocalyptic. Pandemics are not new to this world but the rate at which they are originating raises questions about the factors that are responsible for it. That is where the question of introspection comes. How much are we collectively responsible for in the reshaping of this modern world? Can we really change the loopholes that are existent in the system to create a sustainable future?

Ideally, yes.

Turning away from the journey to the heart of the planet we made, we have embarked on a detour. A divisive detour. The pandemic has rather exposed the fracture lines that have been systemically imbibed in our society. The origin of the virus led to a change in perspective of the world towards Asians as animalistic and it became a subject of hatred. For example, the Singaporean student of Chinese ethnicity who was beaten up by a group of men in London and was told that they do not want Coronavirus in their country. This is just one of the many incidents of anti-Asian hate in Europe and the Americas that has been going on since the start of the pandemic which can be linked to influential global leaders like Donald Trump, ex-President of the USA, who took active part in constantly blaming China for the virus and using racist terminologies. This instinct to humiliate, when it is modelled by someone on a public platform, by someone powerful, filters down into everybody's life, because it gives a kind of permission for other people to do the same thing.

Disrespect invites disrespect. Violence incites violence.

When the powerful use their position to bully others, we all lose. This pandemic has exposed the systemic fracture lines of racism and other forms of hatred magnified to its glory and blowing impetus into people's hearts to portray supremacy over each other. In countries like India, this took an uglier turn as people from the North-Eastern part of the country were attacked in many parts of India and they were accused of being the point of origin for coronavirus in the country simply because of their ethnicity. Political divisiveness along the lines of religion was also observed as Muslims were blamed for the spread of coronavirus.

While we have moved far away in one sense, resorting to nationalist ideologies, far away from globalisation, this pandemic has brought people closer too. The importance of social networking portrayed how closely knitted our interactions are. This fabric of social networking connects us all together and it helps in paving the way to expose and work out systemic problems like racism in our world. One of the great movements that would be considered as a serendipity during this pandemic was the Black Lives Matter' movement. This movement taught us that when we are united, we can uproot the values that erase the morality of this world and bring equality.

In a nutshell, our world is fractured. The winds of change hit the castle in every direction and the tremors of the divisive policies are being exposed radically. The perpetrators behind these divisive policies are taking hold of this rift and magnifying it. We need to identify those fractured lines and seal them. The planet has shown us its healing power when we retract our activities. We need to stop when it is required, and we need to act rationally to provide a sustainable platform for global development.

This pale blue dot on which we stand upon needs a renaissance of equality and sustainability.

LIFE AS A YOUNG ADULT IN SOUTH AFRICA

by Aviwe Gift Ndalana, age 22, South Africa

Let me start by introducing myself. My name is Aviwe Gift Ndalana, a 22-year-old male. I currently reside in a squatter camp in Zwelihle, Hermanus, South Africa. I have been fortunate in my late teens and early adult life to have been part of various non-governmental organizations such as District Six Museum, Great Minds Empire South Africa, and Young and Curious. I served as a young facilitator for District Six Museum from 2014 – 2019, served as a continental member of Great Minds Empire Africa and a President for Great Minds Empire South African chapter for the whole of 2019. I am currently a member of Young and Curious: a group of young people facing, addressing, and trying to teach social issues and mostly mental health through art under pivot collective. I have been and am involved with all the above-mentioned roles and organizations through volunteering. Apart from that, I have a skill and two years of work experience as a software developer.

Being a young adult in these trying times is not easy. We come from different backgrounds, mostly from humble beginnings. The majority of us have, for many years, been victims of poverty. We have memories of our pasts that we do not even want to think nor want to talk about because they bring about suffering and unforgettable memories. So, to say growing up was not easy sounds like a fairy tale to many, but for most of us it is the reality. Most of can and do understand that we are where we are currently because of the sacrifices our parents, uncles, aunties, grannies, and former schoolteachers made just to assist us in advancing our lives for the better. They took up these sacrifices because they have a wish to see us receive better education; something that some of them could not have because of circumstances they faced in the past. They were deprived of many opportunities; the right to be free without intimidation.

Once you reach the stage of being a young adult, you are faced with many personal battles, as well as socially constructed issues that pull you back and add to your troubles. Some of the personal issues you are faced with are your dreams, a life partner, finances, and the future. These may seem like easy battles to fight but, combined with the systems that are there to add more problems for the Black child, most of the time falling seems easier than fighting.

Now adding to these issues is the current pandemic; it is easier for one to fall into depression and/or develop anxiety. Yes, most of our parents have and continue to play very important roles in our lives to see us succeed, so one day we can be in positions of leadership and take this country forward. They have always stressed the importance of education. However, we cannot really say the current education system is there to change and equip a young adult to be independent and succeed, but we can all agree that it is there to train and equip young adults to be submissive and work for the system that has and continues to oppress us.

Unfortunately, things have gone wrong for most of us: we never made it in high school, we became dropouts and added to the challenges the youth are facing. Some of us managed to finish and pass high school but we struggle to get financial backing which often hinders our plans to further our studies. That adds to the challenges as well. A young adult sitting at home when there is a scarcity of jobs, given the high levels of unemployment, makes one wonder if there is even a future to consider; if whether the dreams and careers one wanted to venture into will ever come to life. The downside of being young and unemployed due to illiteracy may lead to one to partake in the wrong things, like criminal activities. Sitting at home and doing nothing because we do not have the right qualifications or the necessary skills to match jobs offers is the biggest challenge we are facing as young people.

There are those who are lucky enough to find finances to go to tertiary institutes and study further and thrive in their respective fields and obtain the qualifications they need and become ready to sell their gained knowledge. They send through their CVs to hundreds of employers and sometimes even lose count of the number of CVs they send. Even then the chances of success are slim because the companies will want someone who has experience. In reality, companies mean business; they simply do not have time to train people because they tend to complain that training new people hinders productivity and is time-consuming. In reality, it is unfair to the young adult graduates to be expected to have work experience. This is also a major challenge: to have qualifications but struggle to find a job because you lack work experience.

In conclusion, it is fair to say that being a young adult in South Africa is not an easy thing and if young adults are not careful, their mental wellbeing can suffer a lot more. Hence it is also fair to call upon society to assist young adults and be lenient with them as they fight huge, unknown fights.

SHARAD SHARMA'S INTERVIEW BY TEAM INDIA (AGE 20-25)

"If you are creating something, if you have something to say, say it loud and clear."

– Sharad Sharma

On a warm winter weekend, we discovered how storytelling can bring about social change by tapping into "Comics Power!" with Mr Sharad Sharma, founder of World Comics Network. Mr Sharma is a cartoonist based in New Delhi, India, who has worked in both print and electronic media for over 25 years. In doing so, he made sure that the voice of the common man reached the mainstream press, and finally the policymakers, through the medium of comics. In the early Nineties he conceptualised the idea of Grassroots Comics and took the art of cartooning to the rural hinterland of India and other parts of the globe. He provided this alternative mode of communication to amplify the voices of the silent majority, by giving them a pencil, paper and hope to sketch-in the change. Mr Sharma believes "ABCD stands for: anybody can draw!".

We spoke to him about his experience with comics, his views on the pandemic, his dreams for this storytelling revolution and everything in between!

Q. Out of all the mediums of communication, why the love for comics?

A. Love for comics because that's the only medium I know and am comfortable with. As for me, I can't be an artist and just create things for self-pleasure and hang it for display in my drawing room, just for myself, for the rest of my life. I think medium is not really important here. Medium is just a means and it's important to understand what you do with the medium. That really makes all the difference.

Q. How has the experience been with the pandemic so far? Do you have any key learnings that you'd like to share with us today?

A. Through grassroots comics, we help people tell their stories, document the stories in their own way, and also reproduce them by simply photocopying them black and white. My job for the last 20-odd years has been to travel across the length and breadth of this country and also across the globe to reach out to people whose voices are probably not getting documented such as homeless people, people living in conflict zones, people living with disability, nomads and so on. We all know what happened due to the pandemic: the whole world halted. We have been doing some work on an online platform, but unfortunately we can't get the same kind of attention and interaction we used to face-to-face and most of my audience is not available on these platforms. The voices of the communities are not being heard because we have a huge digital divide in this country. So it is a great setback for the grassroots comics movement.

Q. How powerful and engaging do you think the tool of storytelling is in giving a voice to the voiceless?

A. Everybody is a good storyteller in this country when you provide them an opportunity. What is really lacking is the medium. So, if there is a medium, they will document the story in a way that they can get the attention of the larger community and hence seek for the solution collectively. In the case of comics, they just have to sit and draw the story, photocopy it and distribute it everywhere. The Grassroots Comics movement encourages participation of the community as these stories are created by local people in local languages on local problems and solutions, featuring local look-alike characters and familiar ambience and the artist is known to them too; he may be living next door! As there is no other mechanism to get the stories of the silent majority of this country, grassroots comics can be the alternative mode of communication or the 'Community Media'.

Q. The urban population mostly knows comics as a medium of entertainment rather than a medium of social change. So, how has the perception and attitude towards comics changed in India, especially with respect to grassroots comics?

A. 90% of my audience have never ever seen mainstream comics in their lives, so for them comics is a four-panel comic poster that they have created, self-published and distributed by themselves. There is still a notion among the urban educated population in India that comics are for children or for the purpose of entertainment, like superhero stories. But comics can also be used as a powerful communication tool. Comics medium came from the West but in a very different shape, size, and format and what we did with comics is to completely revolutionize that idea!

Q. Social issues are known to be very complex, so are these four panels that you're talking about in a grassroots comic sufficient to convey the whole story?

A. During workshops, we suggest participants pick one specific theme or one specific storyline from their life and we tell them "this is going to be your first comic, but not the last one", as they are new creators and may struggle with the theme, or with the process of drawing their story. Also, when you have just a four-panel story, the reading order is simple left to right, top to bottom, there is no confusion. So, it is important from the reader's, as well as the creator's, point of view to be very specific about picking the storyline.

Q. Do you think grassroots comics are both a medium to create dialogue among people as well as a way to deal with trauma through art therapy?

A. Comics are a very non-threatening medium as you just need a paper, pencil, and something to say. There is no kind of pressure, be it from the storytelling perspective or the distribution perspective. Because of this reason, it works very well in conflict regions and around issues surrounding mental health, trauma, and disability as well. For example, just after the 2006 Tsunami, we did a workshop next to the sea with children in Naga Putnam, and this medium brought in lots of stories about the tsunami and how their lives were affected when their village was swept away and so on. It is a beautiful medium that allows you to address very complicated issues.

Q. The Covid-19 pandemic has highlighted the plight of different sections of the society. So, do you think now more than ever we should start telling stories to bring about change? If yes, where do you think we should start?

A. Schools are closed and the media has only been focusing on the number of Covid cases and the vaccine stories while the common people are struggling to survive. Unfortunately, there are issues that are not getting the due attention. I think mass communication should actually be a medium where the masses are involved or where the issues of the masses are getting some sort of representation. It is also really important for active citizens to document these stories on local issues and that's where citizen journalism comes in. In my opinion, each and every active citizen is an activist. We need to come out of our cocoons, interact with people and talk about issues they face, because unless we do that, we won't realise how privileged we are.

Q. We know you've been a journalist and a communicator as well. How do you think we can improve public communication of science and health in India?

A. I think we are struggling with both misinformation and too much information. Most of the time, we don't have the right kind of information. Also, with respect to science communication, I think people mostly find the sciences very boring, until and unless it is really connected to them. In such a case, we can use comics to communicate messages around health and science. I believe that when somebody is just at the receiving end, they won't be interested. What you have to do is engage them and make them part of the communication and let them also tell the stories from their own perspective. In this way, you can help them fact-check while teaching them 'how to tone it down' or 'how to simplify it for the layman', which are also important in science communication.

Q. Grassroots Comics have been giving voice to the marginalized and the previously voiceless for many years now. What potential do you see in this comic movement to scale up in the current as well as the post-Covid world?

A. The Grassroots Comics is not just a medium for self-pleasure, it is a medium for the masses, for the community. It is there to make the development discourses more vibrant and strong, engage the silent majority and bring their point of view on the table. For this to happen, they should also be telling their individual stories. So, I make sure that I'm engaging people and encouraging them to tell as many stories as possible. The future of the comics is going to be 'Comics Journalism', where the comics will become a part of the grassroots-level field reporting. People will tell and document their stories. You name an issue, there should be a pre-existing comic on it. You name a geographical location or language, you should be able to find comic stories in that specific language or dialect. Lack of a medium does not mean that people don't have anything to share, they have lots of different points of views. Unfortunately, these are not being documented or not reaching out to the larger printed form. I can see the future of comics as being more democratic.

The Grassroots Comics movement has introduced comics to the masses as a medium of expression, which lets people decide what issues really matter to them on an individual level. This movement has generated thousands of powerful stories on health, livelihood, education, infrastructure, unemployment, mental health, abuse, domestic violence, trafficking, water crisis, and other such issues — all sketched, published and distributed by the people, for the people. These grassroots stories have managed to initiate dialogue and spark debates on a number of levels. We believe this is a revolution that has the potential to change the world, one story at a time. After all, that's what we call "Comics Power"!

A CONVERSATION THROUGH SPACE AND TIME

by Lucy Porte,
age 19, UK

In an extensive discussion with cultural psychologist Professor Dawn Edge and historian of emotions Doctor Emma Sutton, we delve into the ways that we can learn from different cultures and eras to devise a health system that works better for all.

"It's like we've gone back in time"
— Doctor Sutton.

Historians love their leading questions. One good example at the moment might be: "are we living in good times or hard times?" As a cultural historian, Doctor Sutton has the privilege of being able to dip into the otherwise secret lives of others and can begin to unravel the timeline of human emotions to help us find the answer.

"Death and illness used to be much nearer"
— Doctor Sutton.

It is interesting to think about how changes in healthcare have affected people and their bodies over the years, especially during a pandemic which seems to break down the barriers of time and space themselves, reconnecting us to past times when sickness was ever-present. Doctor Sutton says it is as if the "safety blanket" of Western medicine has fallen down, with previously dependable measures such as vaccines no longer holding up. Professor Dawn Edge agrees, saying this pandemic has "levelled the playing field" geographically too. That is to say, some countries that we can sometimes look down on have so far achieved superior outcomes to ones we see as more advanced (you only need to glance at the statistics for African countries versus those in Europe or North America to see an immediate disparity).

If people's perceptions of physical health have developed over time, our understanding of mental health has practically transfigured. Thirty years ago, when some of today's doctors trained, psychology was a field centred mainly on schizophrenia, manic depression, bipolar disorder, and other forms of psychosis. Now, we're as likely to talk about mental health as mental illness, and self-esteem has become as important as self-discipline. We may be a long way from Victorian ideas of service and sacrifice, but even in living memory there's been a decline in British stoicism and softening of our grandparents' stiff upper lips.

Are these changes in understanding and expectation of behaviour a weakness or a strength? How well placed are we for disaster now, with advanced technology and pharmaceuticals but a strong feeling of security and entitlement towards the magical medicines we get delivered at sci-fi speeds?

"[We need to ask ourselves:] how do we help young people build resilience?" says Professor Edge, and we tentatively discuss how this might be achieved. In times where national services like CAMHS are stretched by misinformed referrals, leading to disappointment for families and increased stress for people further down the list, maybe we should start by looking at the increased pathologisation of reactions to common familial struggles, such as death or parental separation.

This point, raised by one of my fellow interviewers, instantly reminds me of a book my mum gave me called *The School of Life* which asks: with the whirlwind of issues human beings have to put up with, what reason is there really to be sane? Perhaps this revelation could lead to a new era of mental health understanding where we combine the resilience of the past with the realism of today to make a healthcare system that can truly keep up with our times.

Illness casts a dark net over the world which covers borders. Maybe we could do well to look across these apparent partitions in time and space and think about how the people before us would have responded to similar problems, or how those in other cultures do, in absence of all the aids and infrastructure we know now. I hear the phrase "There is no future in the past" thrown around quite a lot, implying there's little point in looking to the past for answers to modern problems. But I think I prefer this motto from Sapienza University of Rome: *Il futuro è passato qui* — "The future has already been here".

*Illustration by
Hanna Gwynn*

WANT TO MEET OUR FULL GLOBAL YOUNG
ADULT EDITORIAL TEAM AND READ
MORE OF THEIR IDEAS? VISIT:

www.planetdivoc91.com

CATCH THEIR CREATIVE FILMS ON WOWBAGGER
PRODUCTION'S YOUTUBE CHANNEL.

TUNE IN TO THE OFFICAL
PLANET DIVOC-91 MIXES AT:

www.mixcloud.com/planetdivoc91

PLANET DIVOC 91

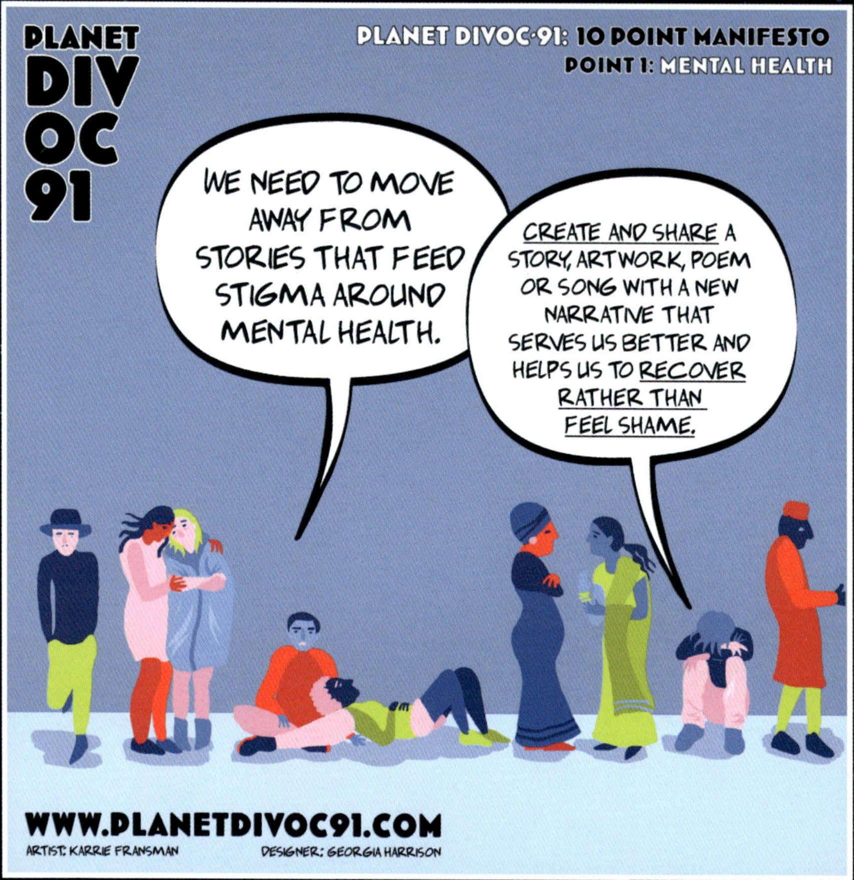

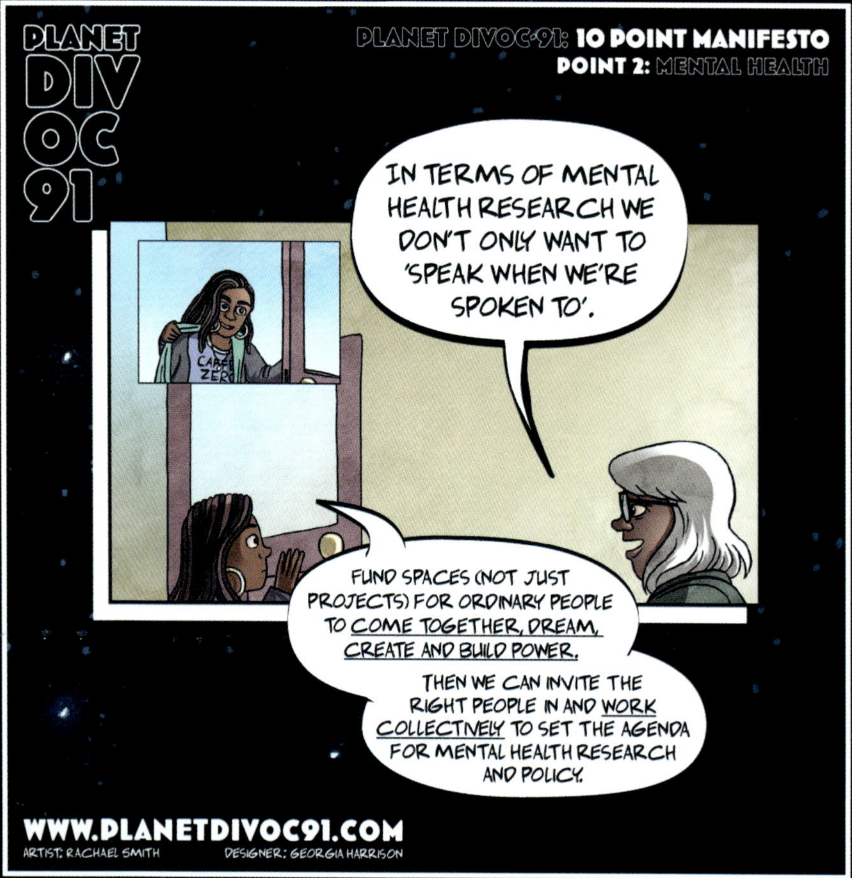

WE NEED TO MOVE AWAY FROM STORIES THAT FEED STIGMA AROUND MENTAL HEALTH.

CREATE AND SHARE A STORY, ARTWORK, POEM OR SONG WITH A NEW NARRATIVE THAT SERVES US BETTER AND HELPS US TO RECOVER RATHER THAN FEEL SHAME.

WWW.PLANETDIVOC91.COM

ARTIST: KARRIE FRANSMAN   DESIGNER: GEORGIA HARRISON

PLANET DIVOC 91

IN TERMS OF MENTAL HEALTH RESEARCH WE DON'T ONLY WANT TO 'SPEAK WHEN WE'RE SPOKEN TO'.

CARBON ZERO

FUND SPACES (NOT JUST PROJECTS) FOR ORDINARY PEOPLE TO COME TOGETHER, DREAM, CREATE AND BUILD POWER.

THEN WE CAN INVITE THE RIGHT PEOPLE IN AND WORK COLLECTIVELY TO SET THE AGENDA FOR MENTAL HEALTH RESEARCH AND POLICY.

WWW.PLANETDIVOC91.COM

ARTIST: RACHAEL SMITH   DESIGNER: GEORGIA HARRISON

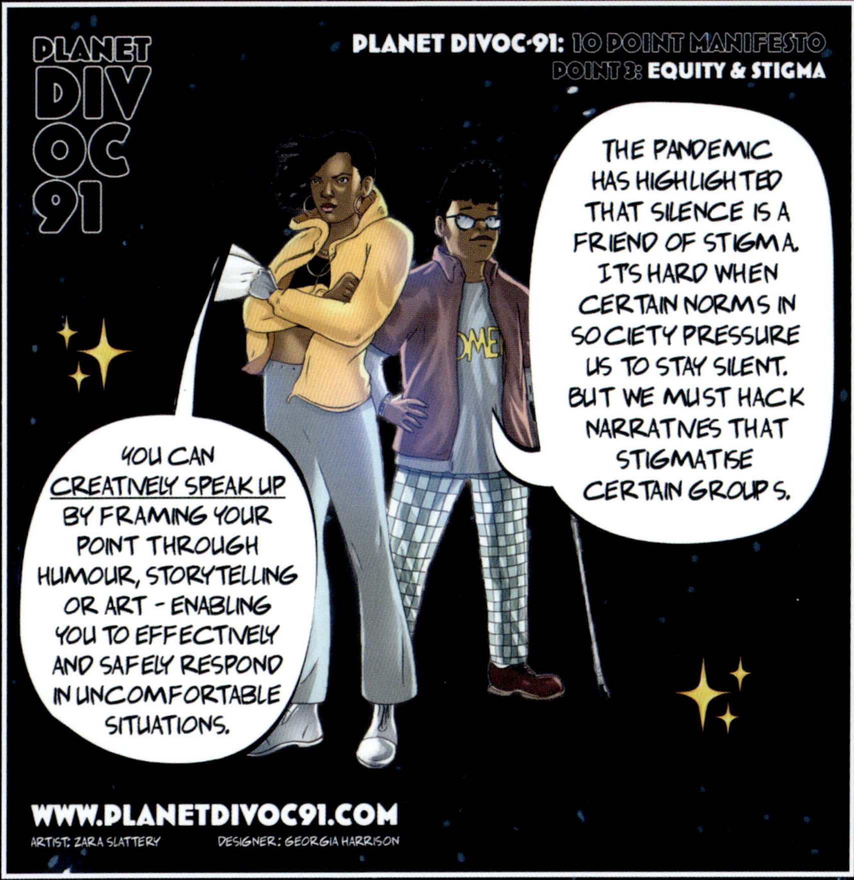

PLANET DIVOC 91

WWW.PLANETDIVOC91.COM

ARTIST: ZARA SLATTERY   DESIGNER: GEORGIA HARRISON

PLANET DIVOC 91

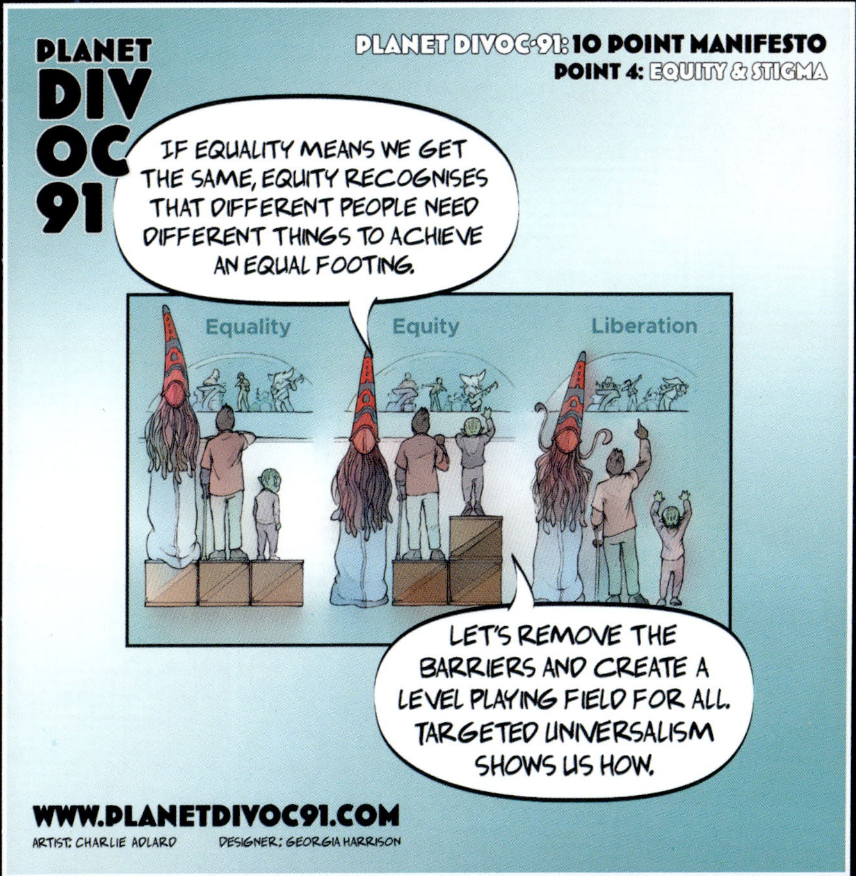

WWW.PLANETDIVOC91.COM

ARTIST: CHARLIE ADLARD   DESIGNER: GEORGIA HARRISON

WWW.PLANETDIVOC91.COM

ARTIST: HANNAH BERRY   DESIGNER: GEORGIA HARRISON

WWW.PLANETDIVOC91.COM

ARTIST: ANAND RK   DESIGNER: GEORGIA HARRISON

PLANET DIVOC 91

WWW.PLANETDIVOC91.COM

ARTIST: CHARLIE ADLARD   DESIGNER: GEORGIA HARRISON

PLANET DIVOC 91

WWW.PLANETDIVOC91.COM

ARTIST: KARRIE FRANSMAN   DESIGNER: GEORGIA HARRISON

PLANET DIV OC 91
PLANET DIVOC·91: 10 POINT MANIFESTO
POINT 9: GENERAL REFLECTIONS
ARE YOU EVEN ASKING THE RIGHT QUESTION?
HOW WILL YOU KNOW UNLESS YOU ASK? NOTHING ABOUT US WITHOUT US.
WWW.PLANETDIVOC91.COM
ARTIST: CHARLIE ADLARD
DESIGNER: GEORGIA HARRISON

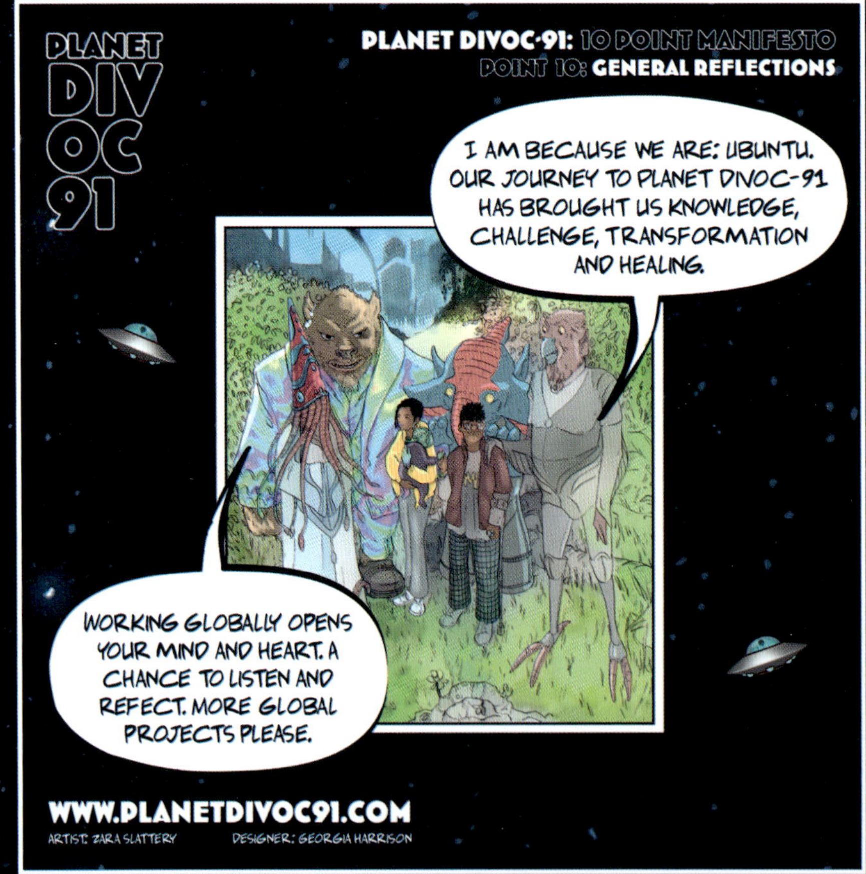

PLANET DIV OC 91
PLANET DIVOC·91: 10 POINT MANIFESTO
POINT 10: GENERAL REFLECTIONS
I AM BECAUSE WE ARE: UBUNTU. OUR JOURNEY TO PLANET DIVOC-91 HAS BROUGHT US KNOWLEDGE, CHALLENGE, TRANSFORMATION AND HEALING.
WORKING GLOBALLY OPENS YOUR MIND AND HEART. A CHANCE TO LISTEN AND REFECT. MORE GLOBAL PROJECTS PLEASE.
WWW.PLANETDIVOC91.COM
ARTIST: ZARA SLATTERY
DESIGNER: GEORGIA HARRISON